TRAIL TO FORT LARAMIE

Jack Latimer has been sheriff of Beaver Creek for ten years. He's content collecting taxes and throwing drunken cowboys out of the saloon on Saturday nights. His Navy Colt is used only to win the annual shooting contest. Then, when the bridge on the trail to Fort Laramie is closed, Beaver Creek explodes into violence as hired killers arrive and ruthless men target Latimer. To survive he'll need to think fast and shoot straight.

JACK EDWARDES

TRAIL TO FORT LARAMIE

Complete and Unabridged

LINFORD
Leicester

First published in Great Britain in 2008 by
Robert Hale Limited
London

First Linford Edition
published 2009
by arrangement with
Robert Hale Limited
London

British Library CIP Data

Edwardes, Jack.
  Trail to Fort Laramie.
  - - (Linford western library)
  1. Western stories.
  2. Large type books.
  I. Title II. Series
  823.9′2–dc22

ISBN 978–1–84782–887–3

Published by
F. A. Thorpe (Publishing)
Anstey, Leicestershire

Set by Words & Graphics Ltd.
Anstey, Leicestershire
Printed and bound in Great Britain by
T. J. International Ltd., Padstow, Cornwall

This book is printed on acid-free paper

1

Jack Latimer swore as the heavy slug sent splinters of rock flying above his head and kicked up dirt among the bunch and buffalo grass. An instant later the sound of the long gun reached him as he scrambled closer to the rock behind which he was sheltering.

'You OK, Mr Latimer?'

'I'm fine, Harry,' he called back to Wilson who was twenty yards away, hidden behind another rock. There was nothing to gain by keeping his voice down. Ned Fuller knew exactly where he was. But did Fuller know where Harry was?

'You keep your head down,' Latimer called again. 'This damned no-good can shoot.'

'What we gonna do?'

'Gimme a minute, Harry. I'm studyin' on it.'

Latimer breathed in deeply. Just what the hell was he going to do, he asked himself. Collecting taxes and chasing brats into the schoolhouse were the toughest jobs he'd faced for a long while. Maybe in the early years he'd had some hard times but a strong arm and ready sidearm had soon won him peace and quiet. Maybe he'd had it easy for too long. Ten years ago he'd have rushed the cabin and shoved a scatter-gun up this no-good's butt. But in those days he'd been out of the army only a few months. Now, he and a young feller in his twenties, who'd put on a badge just a few weeks before, were ducking behind rocks trying to stay off Boot Hill. He filled his lungs with air.

'Ned Fuller! You hear me?'

For a second or two there was only the sound of a bird's distant cry before a shout came from the cabin fifty yards across the open ground.

'Who the hell are you? An' what you after?'

'Sheriff Latimer of Beaver Creek,' Latimer called. 'I gotta posse o' ten men out here. Give yourself up an' I promise you a fair trial down in Cheyenne.'

'You got yerself an' a kid.' Fuller's rough shout didn't hide the sneer in his voice. 'I seen you a mile off. I got men comin' here in a coupla hours. I ain't in the habit o' killin' lawmen but maybe it's time I got started.'

The no-good was bluffing, Latimer was almost certain. As sheriff of Beaver Creek the land around here was within his jurisdiction. The marshal down in Cheyenne would have Fuller hanged for even shooting at a township's sheriff. But should he call Fuller's hand? Both he and Harry Wilson could stay out here for several days if they were forced to. They could pin down Fuller in the cabin until his food, water, and probably his ammunition, ran out. But supposing Fuller wasn't bluffing? Was it worth the gamble?

Harry Wilson was a steady young

man but he hadn't signed on to get himself killed in the first month in the job. If Fuller held the cards he claimed, and his men arrived, he and Harry would be surrounded before nightfall. Latimer risked a look over the top of the rock, ducking quickly, cursing under his breath, as a slug whistled through the air only inches above his Stetson.

'Harry,' he called softly when he'd dropped to one knee.

Wilson, taking his cue from Latimer, kept his voice down. 'Yes, Mr Latimer?'

'I'm gonna make a run for that rock this side of the open ground. If I make it I'm then gonna go for the cabin. You gotta keep Fuller pinned down, an' the second time it's gonna be harder. Reckon you can do that?'

The young man's voice was strained. 'Sheriff, you try that an' you'll get yourself killed!'

'I'm gonna ask you agin, Harry. You reckon you can do that?'

There was a pause. 'I got two

Winchesters here, Sheriff. I'll keep the owlhoot busy.' Wilson missed a beat. 'You get into trouble, an' I'll follow you down.'

Despite the gamble he was preparing to take, Latimer couldn't resist a grim smile. Wilson had steel in his backbone. Even the quiet life in Beaver could sometimes throw up the unexpected. He'd seen his deputy at the annual target-shooting contests, and knew he could shoot, but he'd supposed that when the well-educated Wilson had returned from back East he would join his father and hang up his shingle as one of the town's lawyers.

'Fuller's at the opening to the right of the door,' Latimer called softly. 'I reckon he's not sure where you are.'

'When you're ready to go, I'll make sure he knows.'

'What you plannin' to do?'

'Poke my hat above the rock. He's gonna have to show himself to take a shot at me. Give me the word, Sheriff, when you're ready to go.'

Latimer, wishing he had a scatter-gun, started to check his Winchester before realizing he was wasting his time. Either he reached the rock and the cabin would be within range of his Navy Colt or Fuller would shoot him down as he crossed the buffalo grass. Carrying a long gun might slow him down on what could prove the last run he'd ever make in his life.

He rested the Winchester against the rock and drew his Navy. He pulled out a single slug from his belt. This was no time to have an empty chamber for fear of an accidental shot. The skin tightened over his weather-beaten face as he remembered the crazy French-man in his troop at Pea Ridge. 'You want to live for ever?' he'd shout to the men once Latimer had issued the order to attack. Frenchie had been hit by a Johnny Reb sniper three weeks later, and the sergeant who'd replaced him was never as good. Latimer put his left hand out to steady himself against the rock, his Navy held ready to fire. He sucked air into his lungs.

'Ready when you are, Harry!'

A tobacco-coloured Stetson appeared above the rock over where Wilson was hidden. Immediately, a shot rang out as Fuller fired from the cabin. For a brief moment Latimer saw Wilson's hat fly through the air before he hurled himself from behind the rock. The rapid firing and the ratchet sounds of Wilson loading and reloading his Winchester shattered the stillness of the early summer air. Latimer ran, half crouched, across the buffalo grass. The rock in the middle of the open ground was further away than he'd judged. Its safe haven seemed ever distant, as his boots pounded across the grass, his spurs jingling. His breathing became laboured, sweat running into his eyes. He brought up his arm to brandish his Navy, knowing that at that range only the luckiest shot would hit his target.

He was only six feet from the rock when Fuller must have realized what Latimer was attempting. A slug spurted dirt three feet from Latimer's boots, and he hurled himself forward, landing full stretch behind the rock, his face pressed down on the ground, the tangy taste of grass in his mouth. His heart was beating so fast he thought it might break through his chest.

He gulped in air. So far so damned lucky! He reckoned it was no more than fifteen paces across the open ground. With Wilson on the higher ground and his own position now closer to the cabin, Fuller was faced with threats from different angles. There was a lull in the firing and Latimer scrambled to a kneeling position behind the rock, careful to show nothing of himself to Fuller. Suddenly, three rapid shots came from the cabin. Latimer jerked his head around to look towards where he'd left Wilson. The deputy was out of sight. Had he been hit? Had he showed too much above the rock prompting Fuller's rapid fire?

Latimer pushed himself to one knee, keeping his head down, and unstrapped his spurs. Between shooting, there was a chance that Fuller would hear them as he ran towards the cabin. He looked around to the rock where he'd last seen his deputy. He had to assume Wilson hadn't been hit. Again Latimer filled his lungs with air. One last run, he told himself. If he made it, he'd reach the wall of the cabin.

He took off his hat and waved it from side to side, before ramming it back on his head. He waited, ready to spring from behind the rock and charge towards the cabin. Nothing stirred. Where the hell was Wilson? Then a sudden movement right caught his eye, and he guessed the meaning of Fuller's three rapid shots. The crazy kid must have run from the cover of his rock to three tall cottonwoods way over to Latimer's right, forcing Fuller to shift his aim away from Latimer. There'd never be a better chance of making the cabin.

He burst from behind the rock, his gun-hand held rigid before him. He could see Fuller clearly now at the opening in the cabin, turned in the direction of Harry Wilson, and firing his own Winchester as rapidly as he could. Fuller had pushed open one of the cabin's stout oaken shutters to give him greater protection from the fire that poured down from Wilson's long gun, unaware for the moment of the threat coming at him from across the open ground.

Latimer was only ten yards away from the cabin when Fuller must have realized that Latimer was bearing down on him, and swung his long gun around. Arm rigid, maintaining his pace, Latimer pulled the trigger of his Navy three times. The first slug caught the Winchester, tearing it from Fuller's grasp, the weapon slamming back against the shutter. The second sent splinters of wood spraying over Fuller as he staggered back under the force of the slug. The third found its target, and Fuller howled with pain as he fell out of sight into the interior of the cabin.

Breathing heavily, his gun hand extended, Latimer slowed to a walk, moving cautiously forward. He reached the shutter of the cabin, and stood for a moment against the cabin wall, before swinging suddenly to thrust his Navy through the opening, ready to fire at the slightest movement. Nothing stirred. On the floor of the cabin, Fuller was face down, a bloody stain spreading across his shirt. Latimer saw that his slug had cut a furrow along Fuller's shoulder.

'The doc's gonna patch you up, you sonovabitch,' Latimer said aloud to the groaning Fuller. 'You're gonna be just fine when they hang you down at Cheyenne.'

*　*　*

The townsfolk poured out of stores and workshops onto the boardwalk to see Latimer and Wilson bringing in Fuller to the jail at Beaver Creek. With Latimer in the lead, they rode in single

11

file, Fuller in the middle, Harry Wilson bringing up the rear.

Men dressed in city suits, others in dusty coveralls, a couple of old-timers standing in front of the batwing doors of the saloon with beer mugs in their hands, all cheered the progress of the three riders. Smart ladies in dresses that swept the boardwalk and girls still young enough to have their hair down clapped their hands as Latimer walked his roan along the hardpack of Main Street. On the balcony of Luke Bartram's saloon half a dozen of the calico queens shouted their praise.

'You can have a free one, tonight, Sheriff,' Tess from Texas called out, and the girls screamed with laughter. 'Me, too, Mr Latimer,' another called out, and there was more loud laughter. Several of the ladies on the boardwalk exchanged frowns, tutting loudly their disapproval.

Latimer looked behind him to check that all was well. The outlaw's hands were tied to the pommel of his grey.

Around Fuller's neck was the noose of Wilson's 32 feet of hemp, the dally end secured to the pommel of Wilson's saddle.

'You wanna make a run for it,' Latimer had told Fuller, once they'd lashed him to his own horse. 'You go ahead. Save the hangman down at Cheyenne a job.'

Fuller had spat at him. 'No hick sheriff's gonna keep me in a country jail for one day more than I need to rest up.'

And despite the grim smile Latimer kept on his face as he continued his way down Main Street, acknowledging the shouted congratulations of the towns-folk with a finger to the brim of his Stetson, he knew Fuller could have hit the mark. The cages at the rear of his office were fine for drunken cowboys on a Saturday night. A man like Fuller would take some holding. The sooner the marshal from Cheyenne arrived for his monthly visit in a day or so, and took Fuller away, the sooner he could relax. He drew level with the smithy where Sam Charlton stood in his leather apron, a couple of paces from his anvil, red-hot iron pincers glowing in his hand.

'Sam, I'm gonna need you across the jailhouse,' Latimer called. 'Got some work for you, an' I need it done fast.'

'I'll be there, Sheriff.'

Latimer reached his office and turned his roan's head towards the hitching rail. He stepped down to the hard-pack with an easy motion as the horses ridden by Fuller and Harry Wilson came up to the rail. Fuller sat still, his head up, his hard eyes surveying the press of townsfolk that grouped close.

'OK, everybody,' Latimer called to them. 'Show's over. Any o' you folks wanna join this no-good in a cage?'

There was an excited murmur of noise and the group split promptly, men and women retreating across Main Street, not really believing that Latimer meant what he said. But it was better to be safe than sorry. As Mayor Gibbons

14

had once said, 'Sheriff Latimer can be a mite ornery when he's a mind to.'

Latimer untied Fuller's hands and removed the noose from his neck before stepping up to the boardwalk and unlocking the door. 'Bring him up, Harry,' he ordered. Not waiting, he entered the office and crossed to open a low cupboard. From a deep drawer he took two lengths of heavy chains with shackles attached at each of their ends. He turned as Fuller and Wilson came through the door.

'You goin' yeller on me, Latimer?' Fuller sneered as he saw the shackles.

Latimer ignored him. 'Take him through to one of the cages,' he ordered his deputy. 'We'll shackle this owlhoot to the bars until Sam Charlton fixes things.'

Coarse laughter erupted from Fuller. 'You sure are somethin', Sheriff. Don't you fergit to attend the sewing circle this week!'

Latimer looked at him for a second, his face expressionless. Then he stepped forward quickly and smashed the pointed toe of his boot into Fuller's kneecap. Fuller let out a yell of pain, cursing loudly, as he fell sideways to the floor. Latimer looked down at Fuller who was grasping his knee, his face screwed up in agony.

'You watch your mouth, Fuller, or it's gonna be hard on you for the next two or three days.' Latimer looked at Wilson. 'Grab his other arm, Harry.'

Latimer and Wilson dragged the still cursing outlaw through the door at the rear of the office and along the small passageway to one of the two empty cages.

'Now stand back, Harry,' Latimer said, after they'd heaved Fuller onto the bunk. 'He makes a wrong move while I'm shackling him, an' you shoot him.'

Latimer snapped on the shackles around Fuller's legs and one arm, before leading the length of chain to secure it around the bars of the open door of the cage. He went back to the bunk and pushed his face close to Fuller's.

'You listen hard! I run a decent place here. You'll get three squares, and maybe more coffee when we've a mind to,' Latimer said. 'Doc Mills'll be across to fix you up, an' we'll get you another shirt from your saddlebag. But you give me trouble an' you'll go to Cheyenne in the back of a wagon. You got that?'

Fuller, his eyes burning with hate, stared back at Latimer. He nodded abruptly.

'Let's hear you say it.'

Fuller pulled back his mouth, baring his teeth. 'I got it.'

'We get the next cage ready, an' you'll lose the shackles.'

Latimer backed away out of Fuller's reach, his hand resting on the butt of his Navy, before turning on his heel and following his deputy back into the office. While Wilson went across to the stove and poured coffee into two tin mugs Latimer eased himself down in the chair behind his desk. He blew air through pursed lips.

'Gimme one o' those, Harry, an' take the other to Fuller. Leave your sidearm here.'

Wilson nodded. He drew his Colt and placed it on a table, and picked up the two mugs. 'You reckon Marshal Locke'll be here in a coupla days?'

Latimer looked at the calendar pinned to the wall. 'Maybe three. I'll be glad to get rid of this damned no-good. Soon as the marshal arrives we can take life a mite easier.' He took a mouthful of his coffee feeling the hot black liquid warming his gullet. 'You did just fine today, Harry. I was glad to have you along.'

Wilson, obviously pleased with Latimer's words, went through to the cages carrying the mug for Fuller. As he pushed through the doorway the street door opened and Sam Charlton stepped in from the boardwalk. For a moment his massive build cut through the rays of the midday sun streaming through the open door.

'Sam, the cages need fixin'. I could bust outa there with a butterknife.'

Beads of sweat stood out on Charlton's face. His skin was so black that his high cheekbones looked almost purple. He unwound the towelling scarf from around his neck and wiped his face. His grin was wide.

'Been like that for a while, Mr Latimer. Cowboys you bin puttin' in there couldna handled a butterknife on a Saturday night.'

'Guess you're right, Sam. Town's been a mite quiet these past years.'

'Down to you, Sheriff,' Sam said. 'Reckon Mr Wilson's got himself a good boss,' he added, as the deputy came back into the office. 'I'll get my tools.'

He stood aside as a tall man wearing a grey Prince Albert and an immaculate white Stetson stepped into the office. 'Howdy, Mr Bartram.'

'Howdy, Sam.' Bartram shook his head as Wilson offered him a mug of coffee. 'No thanks, Harry.'

Bartram took the chair opposite

Latimer's desk, a smile showing on his even features. 'Have to hand it to you, Jack. What was it last election year? Little gal you fished outa that old well back of the dry goods store. You swept up the votes of the ladies without drawing breath. I reckon half of 'em woulda made a husband of you.'

Latimer laughed aloud. 'The ladies got their votin' rights, just like you an' me, Luke. Don't know 'bout the other part, though.'

Bartram jerked a thumb in the direction of the cages. 'What was the no-good plannin'? The old silver mine's worked out and ain't worth a nickel, an' it'd take ten men to blow that new safe in the bank. Payroll at the mill ain't due for another month.'

'Fuller ain't a thief, Luke.' Latimer pulled open a drawer in his desk and pulled out a creased and dirty poster. 'Take a look at that.'

Bartram took the poster to read the lines below the artist's rough impression of Fuller's features, before letting out a low whistle. ''Wanted for murder,'' he read aloud. ''Edward Ezekial Fuller, known as Ned Fuller, hired killer and assassin. Five hundred dollars reward if captured alive. One hundred dollars dead.'' Bartram frowned. 'Sounds like some mighty important folks want to see him hang. But what the hell was a no-good like Fuller doin' in these parts?'

Latimer shook his head. 'Beats me. If he hadn't holed up in old Jake Palmer's cabin when Jake was out prospectin' I'd never have known Fuller was around. Jake spotted him in time an' remembered he'd seen this poster the last time he was in here. He was damned lucky he didn't get hisself killed.' Latimer's mouth twisted. 'I'm aimin' to get rid of Fuller as soon as the marshal arrives. Fuller's mebbe got some of his men headin' this way.'

'Then they ain't comin' from Fort Laramie way.'

Latimer frowned. 'I ain't followin' you, Luke.'

'I clear forgot you ain't heard yet. The bridge on the trail is down. I crossed the bridge with the two men I just hired and the engineer closed the bridge behind us. Feller said it'd be out for a week or more. Your marshal ain't gonna be here for a while.'

2

Latimer sat behind his desk thinking he'd hadn't seen as many folks in his office since that day he'd carried Maisie Winslow from the old well to the arms of her mother. All the councilmen were present and alongside Henry Gibbons, the mayor, stood a small man, a brown straw hat held by his side.

Latimer thought Gibbons a pompous son of a gun but he had to admit he'd been good for the town and had rarely caused problems for the sheriff's office. But was he about to start? Gibbons had a look about him that Latimer had seen before, the last time being when he'd tried to have his young son made a deputy. Young Gibbons wasn't a bad feller but the whole town except his pa knew he was happier with his head stuck in a book or taking out his box of water paints and that he jumped like a jackrabbit at the sound of gunfire. Gibbons had taken a couple of weeks to see sense. Latimer stubbed out the thin cigarillo he'd been smoking and waited to hear what all this gathering was about. He didn't have to think too hard to know it was something to do with Ned Fuller.

After a final muttered exchange with a couple of the Citizens' Committee, Gibbons turned to face Latimer. His hands pulled the sides of his grey Prince Albert coat more snugly over his ample stomach, and he arranged his face in what Latimer judged Gibbons thought was a commanding expression.

'We want you to hear what this feller's got to say, Jack.' He steered the small man with the straw hat into a position a pace from Latimer's desk. 'He's got something to say you should study on.'

Latimer looked at the man who was turning his hat in his hands, between running a finger around the inside of his collar. His expression showed that he'd much rather be some place else.

'Andrew Trenchard's my name, Sheriff.'

Latimer nodded. 'Drummer from Cheyenne. You visit the town every coupla months with bags of ribbons an' stuff.'

The small man's eyes popped. 'Never thought you'd noticed me, Mr Latimer.'

'Say what you got on your mind,' Latimer said.

'We're all waitin' on you, Mr Trenchard,' Gibbons said.

Trenchard turned to face Latimer. 'Coupla years back I was workin' down in Colorado in one of them big timber towns. The town wasn't like Beaver with just the one mill. Down there they had two big mills fightin' for business an' things got real nasty between 'em. Loggers gettin' into fights, folks shootin' at each other on Saturday nights after gettin' liquored up. Coupla men from both mills got shot and one night the mill bosses themselves rode into town and took a hand. A fight broke out between 'em and one swore the other would never see another summer.'

'This is mighty interestin' Mr Trenchard,' Latimer said. 'But where you goin' with it?'

'Four weeks later Ned Fuller arrives in town and guns down one o' the bosses. Sheriff puts Fuller in jail, plannin' to wait for the judge. Three days later four of Fuller's men arrive, gun down the sheriff and his two deputies an' Fuller walks outa the jail.'

There was silence in the office for a few moments, the councilmen exchanging glances. Latimer looked across the office to Harry Wilson who looked back at him, his face grim.

'I'm mighty glad you took the trouble to warn us, Mr Trenchard,' Latimer said evenly. 'We'll make sure this no-good Fuller stays here in the jail where he belongs until the marshal gets to town.'

Henry Gibbons stepped forward. 'Jack, you've heard about the bridge. The marshal ain't gonna be here for maybe three weeks.'

Latimer nodded. 'So me an' Harry are mebbe goin' to need some help from Cap'n Bracken an' the Volunteers.'

Gibbons looked around at the councilmen as if seeking their further support. They all nodded their approval and he turned back to Latimer with a set expression on his face.

'We think we gotta better idea.'

'Let's hear it.'

'This ain't just my idea,' Gibbons said. 'We've talked this through.'

Latimer nodded, staring hard at Gibbons. 'Go ahead.'

'Jack, we think you should let Fuller go.'

Latimer leaned back in his chair. 'Now that's a mighty interestin' proposition, Henry, an' why should you gentlemen be thinkin' that?'

'Logic, Mr Latimer, pure logic.' The speaker was a tall man with a beard that reached the top button of his waistcoat. Matthew Epson was the mayor's right-hand-man when he wasn't running the general store.

'Ned Fuller's not a bank or stagecoach robber. He's an assassin. It says that on the notice you got. He's hired to kill folks who get in the way of other folks. Logic tells you there ain't anyone round these parts like that. We reckon Fuller was just passin' through, on his way to the next job.'

Latimer looked at the group facing his desk, his stare resting for a few seconds on each man. 'How's about Mr Danton out at the Lazy T? I'd say he was an important feller, an' the way they say he does business he's bound to have enemies.'

One of the men at the rear made a scoffing sound. 'We all know Josh Danton's got those gunslingers out at the ranch. We mebbe don't like 'em bein' there but it's a fact. Fuller would need an army to get at Mr Danton.'

Gibbons clutched the lapels of his Prince Albert. 'We don't want gunfights in Main Street, Jack. Beaver's a quiet place with decent folk. You keep Fuller here and God knows where it will end.'

'An' folks don't want to see you and Harry on Boot Hill neither,' said one of the men.

Latimer got to his feet. 'When I pinned on this badge all those years ago I swore to uphold the law. Sure, I've had it easy for a while, an' I ain't complainin' about that. But that oath I took means I stay steady through the bad times as much as the good times. Fuller stays where he is until the marshal gets to town.'

'You ain't forgettin' there's an election comin' up soon,' Gibbons said.

'I know that, Henry. I'll do all I can to keep the town peaceful but as long as I'm sheriff I'll do the job my way.'

There was silence in the office for several moments. Then Gibbons stepped forward to glare across the desk at Latimer. 'You're a hard-nosed sonovabitch, Jack,' he said harshly. 'Make sure it don't get you or anyone else in this town killed.'

He turned on his heel and led the councilmen out, the drummer hastily following them through the door and into Main Street. Latimer watched them go. Then he turned to Harry Wilson who had sat silently in the corner listening to the exchanges between Latimer and the mayor.

'What you thinkin' about all that, Harry?'

Wilson twitched his mouth. 'If you'd gone along with the mayor and let Fuller go I'd be reporting you to the marshal in Cheyenne.'

Latimer threw back his head and laughed loudly. 'Then you ain't thinkin' o' turnin' in your badge?'

Wilson stood up. 'I guess you can say that, Mr Latimer. I'm gonna walk over an' see Cap'n Bracken for a couple of his Volunteers — '

He broke off as the door opened. Charley Fairburn from the stage office stood at the door, a puzzled expression on his face. 'Sheriff, we gotta stage headin' this way.'

Latimer frowned. 'Stage came through two weeks ago.'

Fairburn nodded. 'That's right, Sheriff, an' I ain't got this one on my schedule.'

Latimer jumped to his feet. 'Harry, get yourself a long gun, an' round up those Volunteers. I want 'em on top of the livery stable at the edge of town in ten minutes. Then you join me halfway down Main Street.'

Fairburn looked anxious. 'Stage could be a private hire.'

'Sure it could, Mr Fairburn, an' that's most likely the answer, but I ain't takin' chances. I gotta no-good in my cage who could have men 'round these parts. If the stage is no trouble me an' Harry will walk down to the stage office just as if everything is normal. We ain't aimin' to scare decent folks.'

★ ★ ★

Latimer lowered his old brass army spyglass and shoved it into the pocket of his trail coat. He shouted across Main Street, to where Wilson stood, his Winchester at the ready.

'Harry, tell the Volunteers to stand down. Stagecoach is OK. I know the big Swede ridin' shotgun.'

Wilson held up his hand in acknowledgement, stepped out from behind the heavy oak door of the store, and set out for the end of Main Street. The knot of townsfolk who'd been standing inside the store behind him surged out onto the boardwalk, reassured that nobody was going to be shooting at them. Latimer headed for the stage office, glancing around as the stage neared the town, the calls of the driver and the beating of the horses' hoofs reaching his ears.

Five minutes later he stood in front of the stage office as the driver hauled back on his reins and brought the stagecoach to a halt. The big fair-haired man beside the driver shoved his shotgun behind him before climbing down to the hardpack. He touched the brim of his hat in Latimer's direction as he moved to open the stagecoach door.

'Howdy, Sheriff,' he said. 'Guess you're surprised to see us.' A broad smile lit up his weather-beaten face. 'We got ourselves a real good hire job. Folks are headin' for Fort Laramie.'

The Swede opened the door, and held out his arm to assist a woman of maybe forty years to step down to the street. Dark hair showed below a fashionable bonnet and the blue silk of her coat shimmered in the sunlight. 'Take my arm, Mrs Mackie.'

'Thank you, Carl,' she said.

'Ma'am,' Latimer greeted her with a slight pull at the brim of his Stetson. 'Welcome to Beaver Creek.'

The woman had barely moved away from the coach when the figure of another woman appeared at the door. She was in her late-twenties, more expensively dressed than the older woman, and her bright blue eyes shone with pleasure as she looked around and prepared to step down to the street.

Latimer moved quickly past the Swede and extended his arm to her. She looked directly into his eyes, her full lips curving with amusement.

'Do all lawmen in the West have such good manners, Sheriff?'

Latimer grinned. Her soft voice sounded strange after the rougher voices of even the smarter ladies of the town. How many years had it been since he'd heard a Boston accent? 'Only those in Beaver Creek, ma'am,' he said, as she stepped down.

He turned to look at the door again as a distinguished-looking man appeared, a smile showing through his neat grey beard and flowing moustaches. 'I told Miss Emma that the West was not the uncivilized land she'd read about.'

He held out his hand as he alighted from the stagecoach and shook Latimer's hand warmly. 'John Kerswell, Sheriff, and my delightful travelling companions are Mrs Dora Mackie, and Miss Emma Parkes.' He turned as another man stepped from the coach.

'And my secretary, Mr Frederick Turner.'

Latimer exchanged nods with the man who made no effort to shake his hand. Maybe a long journey in the coach had tired Turner. For a pen-pusher, Latimer thought, the man had hard eyes.

'May I ask if you're all heading for Fort Laramie?'

'All except Miss Parkes,' Kerswell said.

'I shall be staying in Beaver Creek for a while. I've business here,' the young woman said.

Behind her, Harry Wilson caught Latimer's eye and raised his eyebrows as Latimer remained expressionless. A young woman with a Boston accent doing business with the men in town was going to be worth watching. Latimer turned to Kerswell.

'I've got bad news, Mr Kerswell. The bridge on the trail is down for mebbe a week. The engineers are working there now.'

Kerswell frowned. 'Then we must stay here,' he said decisively. He looked round to his secretary. 'Please see to all our boxes, Mr Turner.' He turned to the two ladies. 'Of course, you will be my guests at the hotel. No, I insist,' he added as both began to voice objections. 'Your company is all the payment I require.' He held out both arms to them. 'Now shall we inspect the hotel?'

Emma Parkes looked at Latimer. 'Sheriff, I need to discuss my business with you. Is the afternoon suitable?'

'I'll be in the office after my midday meal, ma'am.'

Again he put a finger to his Stetson as Kerswell and the two ladies moved along the boardwalk towards the town's only hotel. He guessed that Jed Morgan, the owner, would be rubbing his hands in a few minutes. He had fancy rooms on the ground floor which he kept for the occasional smart visitor to the town. The rooms would be ideal for guests such as John Kerswell, Turner, and the ladies, and Kerswell was obviously not short of funds.

Latimer stepped down from the boardwalk onto Main Street shoulder to shoulder with his deputy. 'You're a smart feller, Harry,' he said. 'Why would a charming young woman from Boston wish to talk business with a sheriff in Wyoming Territory?'

★ ★ ★

Latimer had taken his meal at the Chinaman's and was in his office writing in his official journal when the door from Main Street opened and Emma Parkes stood on the threshold. Latimer got to his feet.

'Come in, Miss Parkes, but I'm alone. My deputy is about the town.'

'I'm sure I'll be in safe hands, Mr Latimer.'

Her words prompted him to look at her carefully, not sure if she was joshing him. But save for a small curve of her lips she gave away nothing. As she stepped into the office he moved from behind his desk to take a chair from beside the pot-bellied stove and place it before his desk. With a rustle of silk, Emma Parkes took her seat, and placed a leather document case on the floor beside her.

Latimer waited until she'd settled her skirts before taking his own seat, while wondering what business Emma Parkes could possibly have with him. He'd have thought that Harry Wilson's father with his lawyer's shingle hung outside his office would have been a better choice. But he had to admit that sitting opposite this young woman with her fair hair, clear blue eyes, and smooth skin, was no hardship at all. The meeting would probably turn out to be a busted flush, but it had been a while since he'd shared such attractive company.

'How can I help you, Miss Parkes?'

'Twenty years ago, Mr Latimer, my father lived near this town.'

'He must have been an early pioneer. Beaver's only been a town these past fifteen years.'

'He was, but his pioneering was not a success. After fifteen months he left and went back East. He worked hard for many years, and became a very wealthy man.' A shadow crossed her face. 'Sadly, he died last year, and his estate has since been divided equally between my four brothers and me.'

Latimer maintained a look of interest on his face although where Emma Parkes was heading, he had no idea. And why did she need to talk about her private business to him? He was even more convinced she should be talking to Abe Wilson. Emma Parkes picked up her document case and took out a large legal-looking document and rested it on the edge of Latimer's desk.

'I have here, Mr Latimer, papers which show that I am the owner of 160 acres of land within the area of Beaver Creek.'

If Emma Parkes had said that she'd arrived in the town on one of those new velocipedes that he'd read about Latimer could not have been more surprised. He could guess now why she'd come to him first. If the land she owned was already occupied by townsfolk and the law backed her claim then he might just end up having to evict people with whom he'd been friendly for almost a decade. He looked down at the document.

'I think we should see exactly the land you're claiming to own.'

'I'm not 'claiming to own', as you put it, Sheriff,' Emma Parkes said smartly, 'I own it without question. My lawyers have confirmed that.'

'Just my words, ma'am,' Latimer said evenly, noticing how her sharp response had brought a blush to her cheeks. She sure was a handsome young woman. 'Why don't you show me what you have here?'

She opened out the document while Latimer stood up to clear a space on his desk for her. When the document was fully spread out Latimer judged that it was a copy, although obviously done by a skilled draughtsman. Emma Parkes confirmed this with her next words.

'The original is in a Boston bank,' she said. 'I thought it too dangerous to risk carrying it out here.' She placed a long slim finger on the paper where an area had been outlined with red ink. 'That shows the land my father owned and which I have now inherited.'

'Let me get this clear,' Latimer said, frowning. He placed a finger on the document, drawing it along a thin blue line. 'This is the creek to the east of the town.'

'If the creek is still there, yes, that's correct.'

Latimer lowered himself to his seat, looking up at Emma Parkes who remaining standing on the other side of the desk. 'Ma'am, you're gonna think I've forgotten my manners, but I'm gonna tell you. You're plumb crazy!'

'In Boston, Mr Latimer, a lady is not addressed in such a manner!'

'Then you best go back to Boston, Miss Parkes,' Latimer retorted, 'away from our rough manners an' take this paper with you!'

Emma Parkes sat down abruptly, looking straight at Latimer. For a moment he thought she was about to protest angrily again at his words but when she spoke her voice was even.

'Tell me why I'm 'plumb crazy', as you put it.'

Latimer couldn't avoid his mouth twitching. One day Emma Parkes was going to be a real handful for some lucky man. The finer ladies in town would have huffed and puffed at his words, the less fine would have thrown something at him. He put his finger on the area occupied by the land she was claiming to own, or rather, he reminded himself, that she owned without question.

'This land is part of the Lazy T ranch owned by Josh Danton.'

'His cattle may have grazed there,' she said firmly, 'but I shall tell Mr Danton that the land is mine, and I expect him to respect my ownership.'

Latimer was silent for a few moments,

trying to decide how best he could explain the situation. Emma Parkes appeared to believe that the law operated in the Territory the same as back East. Did she think that one of those new-fangled police agents in blue uniforms would escort her? He had to try and put her straight before she got herself into serious trouble.

'Ma'am, Josh Danton rules the Lazy T with an iron hand. He's not gonna give a bent cent for this paper.'

Emma Parkes smiled. 'That's why I've come to you first, Sheriff. I wasn't sure before if I would need the support of a lawman but now I understand that I do.'

For a moment Latimer felt like jumping out his seat and putting this Boston lady across his knee and giving her a good spanking. As it was, he put a hand in the air.

'Stop, ma'am, right there! Josh Danton has a pack of gunslingers who make sure nobody gets too close to the ranch or the cattle. Just this last year they killed three men who they thought were trying to rustle some of the Lazy T steers.'

Her eyes widened. 'And you did nothing about it?'

'That land is outside my jurisdiction. I go out there an' this star I wear means nothing.'

'But is there no law?'

'Sure there is. The law of the gun. OK, one day it'll be different, but not for a while yet.'

'But surely these men wouldn't kill a lady?'

Latimer breathed in deeply. He would have to shock her out of this nonsense. 'No, ma'am. Not at first. They'd keep you alive for a while.' He saw the colour drain from her face, and her hand fly to her mouth. 'I'm real sorry I had to say that, ma'am. They're not words I'd choose to use with a lady. I just want you to understand that life out here is very different from that in Boston.'

He got to his feet as Emma Parkes

stood up. Her face was still pale but her colour was beginning to return and the shock that had shown in her eyes at his blunt warning was fading. Her hands trembled slightly as she folded the document that staked her claim and placed it back in the document case. She buckled the case and appeared to regain her composure. She looked directly at Latimer.

'Thank you for being straight with me, Mr Latimer. I take notice of your advice. But you may be sure I do not give up easily. Good day.'

With a flurry of silk skirts she turned, and before Latimer could move around the desk to reach the door she had gone, leaving behind a faint scent of fresh flowers. Latimer eased himself down on his seat, staring unseeing at the opposite wall. Why would a wealthy lady from Boston travel out West to claim a patch of ground her father had abandoned twenty years before? There was something going on that maybe he should get a handle on or it might just blow up in his face. His eyes strayed to the door that led to the cages as a thought jumped to his mind. Had Fuller been hired to kill Emma Parkes?

3

Latimer was walking his roan back from
the schoolhouse when he heard the
shot. He kicked the sides of the animal
into a lope, ignoring the shouts of the
townsfolk as he headed down Main
Street. As he reached the knot of people
looking up at the boardwalk a few men
and women backed away as if anticipating Latimer's anger.

'Outa my way!'

Latimer's roan scattered the townsfolk as he drew level with Wilson. He
slid from his saddle and mounted the
three steps to the boardwalk as the
deputy, down on one knee, turned to
look up at him, his mouth set. Cradled
in Wilson's arms was a young boy, no
more than eight years old. Blood was
oozing through the bunched cloth that
Wilson held firmly against the boy's
chest. The boy, his eyes wide with

47

shock, stared up at Latimer.

'Doc's on his way,' said Wilson softly.

Latimer felt a great weight settle on his shoulders. He knew from the amount of blood staining the cloth Wilson was holding that there was no chance. As Latimer, too, dropped to one knee, a trickle of blood ran from the corner of the boy's mouth. 'Doctor Mills is comin', son, you just hold on, an' we're gonna fix things.'

He'd scarcely got the words out when the boy appeared to give a choking cough, his eyes closed, and his head fell back. Latimer stood up, his head bowed for a moment as the deputy gently laid the boy down. Behind Latimer came a murmur of noise from the townsfolk, and he spun on his heel.

'The boy's dead! Is that what you folks wanted to see?'

He took a threatening step to the edge of the board-walk, and the nearest line of townsfolk backed away, bumping into the men and women behind them.

'Now go about your business,'

Latimer barked. 'All of you!'

The men and women glanced at each other, and backed away hurriedly, some hastily crossing Main Street to mount the opposite boardwalk, where they remained looking across the street. Others stepped out quickly along the street, casting anxious looks behind, eager to put space between themselves and the angry Latimer.

As they did so, a light buggy came down the street, driven by an elderly man with a mane of grey hair showing beneath his brown derby hat. He leaned back on the reins of the dun-coloured pony and brought the buggy to a halt where Latimer and Wilson now stood alongside each other.

'Is the boy alive?'

Latimer shook his head. 'There's nothing you coulda done, Doc.'

Mills heaved back on the brake lever and got down from the buggy carrying his leather bag. 'Can't remember when we last had a shootin' in this town. Was it an accident?'

'I don't know yet. But I'm damned sure I'm gonna find out.'

Mills stepped up to the boardwalk and looked down at the body. He sighed heavily. 'I've seen him around the town with his pa. He's one of the Jenkins boys from out at the homesteads. Leave him to me, Sheriff. I guess you'll be busy finding out what happened.'

'Thanks, Doc.'

Latimer motioned to Wilson to step down with him. He looked across at the general store on the other side of Main Street. Townsfolk remained clustered around the door. In their centre stood the tall figure of Epson, Gibbons's assistant on the Citizens' Committee, his clothes covered by a long green apron. As Latimer and Wilson headed their way the group broke up leaving Epson standing alone. Latimer and Wilson stepped up to the boardwalk.

'You saw what happened, Matthew?' Latimer asked.

Epson nodded. 'Reckon I did, Sheriff. I'd just come out of the store to help Widow Marvin with a parcel an' I noticed folks walkin' along the boardwalk 'cross the street. Young Jenkins comes skippin' alongside 'em just as the shot rang out, and the poor little critter went down.'

'Did you see where the shot came from?'

'From down the alleyway, I guess.'

Latimer thought for a moment. 'Was the young lady who came in on the stage, Miss Parkes, walkin' near the boy?'

Epson shook his head. 'Didn't see any ladies, only menfolk.'

'Who were they?'

'Couple of the townsfolk but I'd say the nearest were those two gentlemen who came in on the stage, Mr Kerswell and Mr Turner I think their names are.'

Latimer nodded. 'An' what did they do when the boy was hit?'

Epson frowned. 'That was mighty odd. Mr Kerswell moved towards the

51

boy but Mr Turner had his sidearm out. He grabbed Mr Kerswell by the arm and bustled him away. I ran across to see if I could do anythin' an' that was when Mr Wilson arrived an' took charge.'

Latimer nodded. 'Thank you, Matthew. You've been a great help.'

'You think this has somethin' to do with that Ned Fuller?'

'Killin' a boy don't make much sense, Matthew, but I'll find out.'

Latimer turned and went down the steps to the hard-pack followed by Harry Wilson. When they were out of earshot of the townsfolk who had again appeared near the general store Latimer turned to his deputy.

'I'll get my horse and go back to the office. You go to the hotel and bring Turner back with you.'

'What if he's busy with Mr Kerswell?'

'Then grab him by the ears and drag him. I've got questions for that feller an' I'm gonna get some answers.'

Latimer had reached the other end of

the street when he saw Henry Gibbons standing outside his office door staring towards him. He reached the hitching rail outside his office and slid from his saddle to secure the reins. Gibbons didn't give him a chance to reach the boardwalk before letting fly.

'You satisfied now, Jack? There'll be tears tonight at the Jenkins homestead with the boy cold in the ground. I warned you what would happen. You're gonna have that boy's death on your mind for the rest of your life!'

'I'm not responsible for the boy's death,' Latimer said evenly. 'Whoever pulled the trigger is to blame.' He stepped past Gibbons and pushed open the door to his office. 'But I'll tell you somethin', Mayor, I'm gonna find out who did it, an' see him hang.'

'You give me your word on that?' Gibbons barked.

'I give you my word. Now I got work to do.' Latimer turned away and closed the door in Gibbons's face.

Twenty minutes later Latimer was

behind his desk writing his report of the events of the last hour or so. When the marshal arrived he'd want to inspect the notes and it was important, should there be a trial, that all the facts were recorded as accurately as possible. He put down his pen and looked up as the door opened. Turner stepped into the office closely followed by Harry Wilson.

'I'm a busy man, Sheriff,' Turner said brusquely. 'I don't take kindly to be rousted out of my hotel room by your deputy.'

Wilson stepped forward, carrying the chair he'd picked up from beside the pot-bellied stove. 'Take a seat, Mr Turner.'

'I ain't sittin' down, son, 'cos I ain't stayin'.'

Wilson slammed down the chair and took a couple of paces to push his face close to Turner's. 'You wanna address me, Mr Turner, you use Deputy or Mr Wilson. Just 'cos you're out West you ain't with hayseeds. Mr Latimer, here, was a lieutenant in the Union Army. I studied law back East for three years. We both know the law in this Territory, an' you'd better learn some mighty fast. You try an' duck our questions 'bout that boy's shootin' an' you're gonna end up in a cage. You got that?'

Turner, his face taut, glared back at Wilson for a few moments. Then, with a wave of his hand that had the sun glinting on the gold ring he wore on the little finger of his left hand, he gave a brief nod.

'You've made your point, Mr Wilson,' he said. 'Guess I made a mistake there.'

Showing no signs of being disconcerted, he turned to face Latimer who'd been watching the action with amusement showing in his grey eyes. 'You've got questions for me, Sheriff,' he said, lowering himself to the chair.

'Mr Turner, you've a Colt on your hip. I saw the cloth fold on that fancy coat as you sat down, an' I guess you're carryin' a derringer. You doin' much pen-pushin' work with those two?'

'I gotta pen for that, Sheriff.'

'Somebody took a shot at you or Mr Kerswell. They hit the boy as he was skippin' past. So this is about me knowin' which one of you was the target.'

Turner raised his eyebrows. 'Seems as if Mr Wilson wasn't talking outa turn,' he said. 'Nobody was shootin' at me,' he said.

'You sure old enemies haven't caught up with you?'

'My old enemies are all on Boot Hill.' A smile flickered for a second on Turner's face and then was gone. 'I reckon some no-good was tryin' to kill Mr Kerswell,' he said. 'If you ask me to guess I'd say it was a damned gunslinger by the name of Ned Fuller.'

'That could be a mite difficult for Fuller, seein' as he's back in one o' my cages.'

'Jesus!' Turner looked round at Wilson and then back to Latimer. 'You two fellers really are somethin'.'

'So you're hired to keep Mr Kerswell alive. Is that it?'

Turner nodded. 'Mr Kerswell's a senior government man. He's been tasked to carry out an enquiry throughout the Territory.'

Latimer frowned. 'What sort of enquiry?'

Turner shook his head. 'I can't answer that. I know he meets land agents, surveyors, lawyers, those sorts of fellers. Sometimes he has me ride out across open ranges with him. We've been in half a dozen parts of the Territory these last eight months. He's talked to the Shoshone with the help of a feller from Cheyenne. But I don't know exactly what he's about. I asked him once an' he told me it was better I didn't know.'

'Any idea how this could affect Beaver Creek?'

Turner shrugged. 'I don't know that it does. I believe we're only here because the bridge is down. An' the sooner we get our escort of soldiers from Fort Laramie the sooner I'm gonna sleep easier. You might be holdin' Fuller but he'll have men around. One of 'em must already be in town. But not only will they be tryin' to kill Mr Kerswell, they'll be tryin' to get Fuller outa your cage.'

'The ladies you're travelling with,' Latimer said. 'What do you know about 'em?'

'We ain't really travelling with them. They were at the last stage station where we changed horses an' were gonna wait for the regular stage. Then Mr Kerswell got a mite impatient an' we picked up the hired coach. You've seen Mr Kerswell, he has an eye for the ladies. When he heard they were plannin' to travel this way he offered them seats in our private hire.' Turner's mouth twisted. 'Miss Parkes is too much a feisty young gal for a feller like me. Mrs Mackie sure is handsome, though.'

'I know why Miss Parkes is here. How about Mrs Mackie?'

'Lost her husband five years ago, so she said. She's joinin' her brother at Fort Laramie.'

'We could provide a couple of Volunteers, give you a hand to look after Mr Kerswell,' Harry Wilson said.

Turner appeared to think for a moment. 'I appreciate that offer, Mr Wilson, an' I may have to do that. When I'm ready for them I'll let you know.' He turned back to Latimer. 'Do you know how long the bridge will be down?'

'The engineer's gonna send a messenger when he's got it fixed.'

Turner got to his feet. 'Then I'll get back if there are no more questions.'

'Not for now, Mr Turner.'

Turner picked up the chair and replaced it alongside the stove. 'You ever think of coming back East, Mr Wilson, the government can always find a job for a useful man,' he said.

'Good of you to say so, Mr Turner,' Wilson said. 'But I guess I'll be hanging my shingle up one day in Beaver when Pa reckons he wants to quit.'

Turner nodded. 'Good day, gentlemen.'

After Turner had closed the door behind him Wilson got up from his seat to cross to the stove. He took down a couple of tin mugs from the pegs on the stucco wall close by and poured the hot black liquid into the mugs from the coffee pot. He brought one across to Latimer who had remained behind his desk.

'Thanks Harry,' Latimer said. 'I reckon you impressed that government man.' He took the mug from Wilson's outstretched hand. 'Who d'you reckon are the two best Volunteers aside from Cap'n Bracken?'

'Two fellers we put on top o' the livery stable,' Wilson said promptly. 'Charlie Wilkins and Dutch Holland.'

'OK, you go see 'em. Explain we want a watch on Fuller night an' day. Tell 'em I'll see the mayor, make sure they get a bounty. You reckon they'd be willin' to go along?'

Wilson grinned. 'They'd keep watch on the devil if it meant they didn't have to work at the saw-mill for a spell an'

60

still got paid.' He took his hat from a peg. 'I'll go see them now.'

Latimer took down his own hat and left the office to walk across to the newspaper office where he knew he'd find Henry Gibbons. The meeting, he knew, would be difficult after their confrontation on the steps of his office. But it was unreasonable to ask Wilkins and Holland to give up their wages from the mill to guard Fuller without the town finding the money they would have earned.

He pushed through the door of the *Beaver Clarion* and saw Gibbons, a white apron protecting his clothes, standing beside the huge metal printing machine giving instructions to the grey-haired man who'd worked in the office ever since Latimer had first arrived in Beaver. Gibbons turned as the bell on the door jangled above Latimer's head.

'Sheriff,' he greeted Latimer abruptly.

'I need to tell you something,' Latimer said, his eyes resting for a moment on the grey-haired man alongside Gibbons.

'Fred, why don't you carry on with that job out back for ten minutes or so?' Gibbons said.

'Sure, Mr Gibbons,' the man said.

Latimer waited until he and Gibbons were alone before he spoke. 'Fuller has been hired to kill John Kerswell.'

Gibbons frowned. 'So what makes Kerswell so important?'

'He's a senior official from back East. Turner is a government agent acting as Kerswell's bodyguard.'

Gibbons screwed up his mouth in dismay. 'If we'd released Fuller . . . ' His voice trailed away.

'Kerswell would probably be dead by now,' Latimer said. 'Turner's told me Kerswell is holding an inquiry into the Territory but he doesn't know the details.'

'My God! Is the town involved?'

'Turner thinks not.'

'We run an honest town here,' Gibbons said. 'But if Kerswell is killed while he's in Beaver it will be terrible.'

Terrible for your political ambitions, Henry Gibbons, thought Latimer, but decided not to say it. Instead, he saw his chance for the Volunteers.

'I need to hire Wilkins and Holland of the Volunteers. They'll have to give up their wages at the mill.'

'Anything or anyone you need, Jack. The town will pay,' said Gibbons promptly. 'But no more than they'd get at the mill,' he added.

Latimer nodded. 'Kerswell's expecting an army escort to Fort Laramie but I reckon they'll wait until the bridge is fixed.'

'We've got to keep Kerswell alive until the soldiers arrive.'

Latimer nodded. 'I'll make sure we do.'

He was aware that Gibbons's eyes were boring into him as he turned and left the office. He hoped he hadn't made a promise he couldn't keep.

He was back at the door of his office about to enter when he saw Emma Parkes approaching him along the boardwalk with a serious look on her face. He'd been pleased to learn that she wasn't the target of the unknown gunman but right now an argument about her land claim was something he could do without. He pushed through the door into his office half hoping she'd walk straight past but it wouldn't be too hard on him if she did decide to call. He was hanging up his hat when the door opened behind him, and he turned around. For a moment before she stepped forward the sun outlined her figure. She sure was a handsome woman. Normally he'd like nothing better than to share her company for a while but he had other problems on his mind. He held up his hand.

'I'm sorry, Miss Parkes. You'll have heard about the shooting. This is no time for me to talk about your land claim.'

She stepped into the office, her silk skirts rustling, her buttoned shoes sounding on the boards. 'I'm not here about my land, Mr Latimer. I saw the man who shot the boy.'

4

Latimer stood very still for a moment. Then he crossed to the wall to pick up the chair from beside the stove. He placed it in front of his desk, and took his own seat, studying the young woman while she adjusted her skirts. She raised her head and he half expected she would turn her head and look away but she sat quite composed, returning his gaze.

'What took you so long, Miss Parkes?'

'I'll be honest with you, Sheriff. I thought long and hard about coming forward. I do not wish to be diverted from my business here and I'd assumed that some of the townsfolk would come forward.'

Latimer shook his head. 'If anyone had seen what happened I'd have been told by now.' He paused, and again held the young woman's gaze. 'How come among all the townsfolk you're the only one who saw what happened?'

'My room overlooking Main Street is noisy. I'd gone upstairs to find out if a room there would be quieter before I spoke with Mr Morgan. I was in the passageway, when I saw through the window a man in the alleyway across the street. He seemed to be acting strangely, and I stopped to see what he was doing.' She paused, as if recollecting what she had seen. 'He opened a door on the side of one of the buildings and stood behind it.'

Latimer frowned. 'How did you know he hadn't gone into the building?'

'He didn't fully disappear from my view. He stood half hidden as if waiting for something across the street.' Emma Parkes pushed out her lips. 'I was intrigued by what the man was about, and I stayed by the window.'

'Then what happened?'

'A few minutes passed by and suddenly he stepped from behind the door with a gun in his hand. I heard the shot from the open window, and there was shouting below me from several men. I saw the man turn and run around the end of the building and out of sight.'

'A boy was killed,' Latimer said.

Emma Parkes bit her lip. 'Yes, I've been told.'

'Did you recognize the man?'

'No.'

'Can you describe him?'

'He was a tall man, dressed in range clothes, about thirty years old. He wore his boots like a cavalry man.'

Latimer reckoned that description would fit about a third of the men in Beaver and the homesteads to the west of the town before he even began to think about the ranch hands and the owlhoots out at the Lazy T.

Emma Parkes put a finger to her lips. 'I've remembered something. He had silver markings on the front of his boots, a single line on each boot, curling like a snake.'

67

Latimer froze. Jesus Christ! 'Are you sure about that?'

'Yes, I'm sure.'

'Have you told anyone else this?'

She shook her head. 'No, I thought you should hear it first.'

'That was good thinking, Miss Parkes.'

He looked directly at her eyes. Hell, if he thought she wouldn't scream for help he'd have leaned across the desk and taken her hand. Anything to convince her of the importance of what he was about to say.

'You must say nothing of this to anyone.' He leaned towards her across the desk. 'Tell nobody, d'you understand?'

Her eyes widened. 'Goodness, Sheriff. Do you know the man?'

'Yes, I think I do.'

'Are you able to tell me?'

Latimer shook his head. 'You'll learn soon enough. But think what I've said. Do I have your word that you'll keep silent?'

'If you insist. But why the need for secrecy?'

To keep you alive, he almost said. Instead he repeated his request.

'I'm askin' you agin. Do I have your word, Miss Parkes?'

She hesitated for a few seconds, and then nodded. 'You have my word, Mr Latimer.'

Latimer stood up as she began to rise. This time he was quick enough to get around his desk and escort her to the door. After he'd bid her a good day and closed the door he stood for a moment turning over in his mind what his next move was going to be. Then he went to his desk and picked up his pen.

★ ★ ★

'Wilkins and Holland will be here at sundown,' Harry Wilson said. 'I've tol' them what we need, an' they'll work out a routine so one of 'em is always on guard.'

'The town will pay them,' Latimer

said. 'Give 'em each a scatter-gun an' plenty o' buckshot. I don't want hand-guns anywhere near the cages. Now take a seat, Harry. We've got some thinkin' to do.'

A puzzled expression on his face, Wilson took the seat vacated by Emma Parkes. 'You sayin' we got even more problems?'

'I know who shot the Jenkins boy.'

Wilson sat up straight. 'How the hell — ?'

'I've got someone who saw the shootin', an' identified the sonovabitch,' Latimer cut in. 'You'll have to trust me on this, Harry. I'm not tellin' anyone who my witness is.'

Wilson shifted his eyes to look out of the window overlooking Main Street, appearing to turn over in his mind what he'd been told. At last, he looked back at Latimer. 'You have your good reasons, I guess,' he said slowly. 'But what happens if — ?'

'If I get killed,' Latimer interrupted. 'There's paper in the safe with the name of the witness. You take it from there.'

'OK, who we goin' after?'

'Will Danton, Josh Danton's son.'

Wilson leaned back in his chair, his mouth open. 'Now hold on,' he said, when he'd got over his surprise. 'Why would he be tryin' to kill Kerswell?'

Latimer shook his head. 'I don't know. But we ain't gonna turn a blind eye 'cos he's a Danton. We're gonna have to put him in a cage.'

Wilson looked across the office at Latimer, pursing his lips in a silent whistle. 'Sheriff, I ain't been with you all that long, but I'm hopin' that you trust me.'

'I trust you,' Latimer said.

'Puttin' Will Danton behind bars is gonna cause a lotta trouble. Not just for you an' me but mebbe for the whole town. If I'm to stand with you then I have to know the name of the witness.'

Latimer was silent for several moments. He guessed that if he insisted on Wilson's blind loyalty the deputy would go along. His father had served in the artillery during the war and Wilson would be aware of the need to obey an order. An owlhoot like Fuller behind bars was enough trouble for a small town like Beaver. The son of the most powerful man in the county alongside him would bring a heap of trouble. Wilson was right. If he was putting his life on the line, he had a right to know.

'Miss Parkes is the witness,' he said.

Wilson leaned back in his chair, disbelief showing on his face. 'How could she recognize Will Danton? She's only been in town a few days.'

'She described the silver markings on Danton's boots. Nobody else in the whole Territory, I reckon, has boots like those.'

Wilson frowned. 'You ever thought she could be playin' a clever game?'

'I ain't followin' you.'

'You tol' me she has the land claim on the Lazy T spread. Maybe she's seekin' some sort of a deal. I reckon behind that young woman's pretty face she's as smart as a whip.'

The thought chased through Latimer's mind that his life was suddenly going to hell in a handcart. Less than a week ago he'd been thinking about the chances of his re-election and what he'd do if a rival garnered more votes. Now he was backing his judgement of a young woman he'd known only a few hours; he'd got the threat of gunslingers breaking out Fuller, and he was about to enrage Josh Danton.

'Miss Parkes ain't a liar. I've told her to keep her mouth shut, an' we're going to keep her name between us.'

'We could have a problem with that,' Wilson said.

Latimer frowned. 'How d'you mean?'

'Will Danton gets himself a lawyer, an' I think he can demand to know the name of the witness. I'd need to check my books but I'm sure that's the position.'

'OK, we keep quiet until someone speaks up.'

Wilson looked across the room for

several seconds, before he nodded.

'OK, what we gonna do?'

'Is Will Danton still in town?'

'He's over in the Dollar. I saw him talkin' with Luke Bartram afore he went in.'

'Any of those owlhoots from the Lazy T with him?'

'A couple, I guess. One of 'em's that big feller who favours Californian spurs.'

Latimer knew who Wilson meant. Frank Armand ran the gunslingers Josh Danton paid to deal with rustlers and anyone else who thought they could take a piece of the Lazy T. Latimer had come up against Armand when the bunch of no-goods first joined Danton's payroll. They'd piled into Luke Bartram's saloon one Saturday night and made trouble. Latimer had called on a few of the Volunteers and with their help stuck the whole bunch in cages. In those days the locks on the cages were fine. The no-goods had made a racket loud enough to wake the town until Latimer and a couple of the Volunteers had thrown buckets of cold water through the bars.

'Beaver's a quiet place,' he'd said when Armand arrived the following day to find out why his men hadn't returned to the Lazy T. 'Folks don't take kindly to drunken fights spilling over onto Main Street. Those owlhoots are stayin' where they are unless you fancy payin' their fines. I'm postin' 'em all for a month. They show their faces in town afore then an' I'll have 'em breakin' rocks down in Cheyenne.'

'You sayin' my men cain't ever come into town?' Armand had said.

'After a month they're free to come into Beaver but they don't make trouble. You make sure they know that.'

Armand had paid the fines, and told his men to get the hell back to the Lazy T. In the street, his face grim, he'd watched them shuffle off towards the livery to pick up their horses. As he'd been about to mount his horse he'd turned back to Latimer.

'Shootin' at lawmen gets a man hung where I come from,' Armand had said. 'We don't want to cross each other agin.'

Latimer hadn't seen Armand since that day. Some of his men paid regular visits to the saloon but Armand never showed, although Luke once said that Armand paid Texas Tess to go out to the ranch a couple of times a month. So why had Armand chosen this time to visit the town? Had he heard of Emma Parkes's claim or was this connected with Fuller and Kerswell?

Latimer stood up behind his desk. 'Get yourself a long gun, Harry. This is what we're gonna do.'

★　★　★

Latimer pushed through the batwing doors of the Silver Dollar. There was nothing unusual about the saloon, aside from maybe its size. He'd been in a dozen smaller ones like it on the trails to Fort Laramie and Cheyenne. Over to his left the long bar stretched to the staircase that led up to the rooms where Luke kept the calico queens. On the wall over to the right a long mirror was pinned, helping to make the place look bigger.

Against the back wall a raised platform provided space for the fiddlers who played on a Saturday night. A mixture of long tables and smaller tables for cards stood on the plank floor covered with its thin layer of sawdust. Luke Bartram was standing at the bar his back to the door talking with the barkeep. The man spotted Latimer and said something to the saloon owner. Bartram turned to face Latimer.

'Howdy, Jack. A mite early but there's a bottle for you here.'

Latimer stepped into the saloon keeping his eye on the only other three men in the saloon. They'd glanced up from their cards for a moment when he'd pushed through the batwing doors but now appeared to be concentrating on their game.

'I'm workin', Luke,' Latimer said.

He strode to the rear of the saloon, his eyes on the silver markings of the boots that showed beneath the table. He stopped a pace from the three men who looked up from their cards. Will Danton was flanked by Frank Armand and another man he didn't recognize. Armand looked up, a frown on his face.

'You got somethin' to say, Sheriff? You're bustin' in on our game.'

'Will Danton, I'm arrestin' you for the shootin' o' the Jenkins boy.'

With a muttered oath the man to Latimer's right pushed back his chair, his hand dropping to his sidearm. With practised ease Latimer drew his Colt and struck the man across his face, sending him sprawling from his chair to the sawdust where he lay still. Almost in the same movement he'd swung back to bear on the other two. Neither Danton nor Armand had moved. Muffled cries of alarm came from Luke Bartram and the barkeep behind him. Danton still had cards in his hand, and he placed them on the table before him.

'Have you lost your mind?'

'I have a witness who recognized you, Danton.'

Armand glanced at Danton alongside him. 'Guess this was always gonna happen, Will. Me and Latimer, I mean.' He turned back to Latimer. 'You ain't makin' sense, Latimer. Why would Will kill a boy?'

'I ain't interested in reasons.'

Armand made a show of looking around the saloon. 'You're alone, Latimer. Your pal Bartram sure ain't gonna help you. Why don't you back off, an' take some time to think what you're doin'?'

From behind and above Latimer came the ratchet sound of a Winchester preparing to fire. 'Two of us, Armand, an' you're plumb in my sights,' called out Wilson from his position on the balcony. 'One of you makes a wrong move, an' I'm gonna shoot you both down.'

There was silence in the saloon for a second or two. Armand's face tautened, and he moved his hands slowly onto the surface of the table where Latimer could see them.

'Seems you ain't the hick sheriff I took you for, Latimer,' he said. 'But you're makin' a big mistake. Josh Danton's gonna destroy this town if you put Will in jail.'

'I'll take that chance.' Latimer took a step back. 'On your feet, Danton.'

'An' if I don't?' Danton said.

Wood splinters flew from the plank floor two inches away from Armand's chair as in the same instant the report of Harry Wilson's Winchester sounded around the saloon.

'A warning,' said Latimer. 'I'll not tell you agin, Danton. On your feet.'

Armand stared hard at Latimer. His eyes flickered up towards Harry Wilson's position on the balcony. 'Best do as he says, Will,' Armand said eventually. 'Don't you worry none. We'll soon have you outa this.'

★ ★ ★

Harry Wilson stepped back into Latimer's office from the passageway fronting the cages. 'Damned good job Sam fixed both cages,' he said wryly. 'Didn't expect we'd need both of 'em so soon.'

'Go back to the saloon, an' check on Armand,' Latimer said, looking up from the book he was writing in. 'He ain't likely to do anythin' crazy but I'm gonna be happier if he's outa town.'

Wilson looked at Latimer. 'I sure didn't reckon on this much excitement when I put on the badge.'

'Goes with the job, Harry. We just gotta make sure we stay alive.'

'I'll drink to that,' Wilson said with a grim smile, 'when the town's back being peaceful.'

He left the office and Latimer picked up his pen again. For the best part of fifteen years the place had been quiet with decent hardworking folks going about their business. Now he felt as if he was living in a cattle town like Abilene. How the hell did lawmen sleep in a place like that? He looked up as the door to the street opened. Emma Parkes stood in the threshold. Latimer got to his feet.

She stepped into the office a determined look about her. 'I saw the man you've just brought out of the saloon. That's the man I saw shooting from the alleyway.'

Latimer was about to reply when behind Emma Parkes the street door burst open. Henry Gibbons stormed into the office, ignoring Emma Parkes who stepped back hurriedly to avoid being trampled. Gibbons halted in front of Latimer's desk, his face puce with anger.

'Have you gone out of your mind? Have you gone stark, staring mad? What the hell d'you mean putting Josh Danton's son in jail for the shooting of the Jenkins boy?'

'I have a witness who saw him do it.'

Gibbons swung around to face Emma Parkes. 'A witness!' he roared. 'A damned witness! Young lady, you've been in this town for only two days.

What the hell d'you think you're doin'?'

'Who said Miss Parkes was my witness?' Latimer said quickly.

Gibbons swung on Latimer. 'Then what the hell is she doin' here? You tell me that.'

Latimer thought fast. 'Miss Parkes and I are talkin' about a buggy ride we're takin' together.' He looked across at her. 'Shall we say ten in the morning tomorrow, Miss Parkes?'

Behind Gibbons her eyes opened wide as she looked past the mayor's shoulder in Latimer's direction. Indecision showed for a second in her eyes, and then she nodded. 'That would be very suitable, Mr Latimer. I shall expect you then.'

Gibbons turned to face her, his face still red but this time showing more embarrassment than anger. He gave a brief bow. 'I apologize for my manners, Miss Parkes, and my unseemly language.' He forced a weak smile. 'You must understand, ma'am, these are trying times for Beaver Creek.'

'I understand, Mr Gibbons. Your apology is accepted.' She gave a short nod. 'Gentlemen,' she said.

She turned, and Gibbons moved quickly to open the street door, bowing again as she stepped out onto the boardwalk, and closing the door quietly behind her. Latimer remained expressionless, thinking not for the first time that Emma Parkes was proving a real handful. Gibbons came back to the desk, and took the seat. The polite manner he'd shown a few moments before with Emma Parkes had vanished.

'Now you listen to me. I'm the mayor of this town, and it's the town that pays you. You ain't on a holiday here. Goin' buggy rides with a pretty gal is mighty fine but when you got Fuller an' now Will Danton behind bars it ain't makin' much sense.'

'It does if I can find out what the hell's goin' on in this town.'

'Fuller's hired to kill Kerswell,' Gibbons snapped. 'You've told me that.'

'So why would Will Danton try to kill Kerswell?'

'How the hell do I know? An' what's this got to do with that young woman?'

'She's got a claim on Lazy T land,' Latimer said.

Gibbons' jaw dropped. 'My God! You sure of that?'

'I've seen the documents. That's what the buggy ride's about. I'm hopin' I'm gonna learn a lot more.'

Gibbons pulled out a large red and white spotted handkerchief and mopped his forehead. His anger had melted away to leave him with a desperate note in his voice. 'This is gonna finish us. Cheyenne's gonna wish the town would just disappear.'

Latimer shook his head. 'We keep Kerswell alive, we hold onto Fuller, and you show that no man is above the law. The governor himself will be ridin' outa Cheyenne to shake your hand.'

Gibbons lowered his handkerchief slowly, a thoughtful expression on his face. For a moment he looked almost pleased, and then his face darkened. 'Josh Danton ain't gonna see his son facin' a trial for shootin' a homesteader's boy. He'll pay off Jenkins.'

Latimer's face hardened. 'Josh Danton can give Jenkins as much money as he's a mind to. His son murdered a boy in this town an' he's goin' before a judge.'

Gibbons's anger reappeared. 'You keep talkin' like that an' Josh Danton will send in his gunslingers. You an' Wilson got enough to worry about. It don't make sense to ask for more trouble. An' I'm telling you now, this town's got no hankering for gunfights down Main Street.'

Gibbons didn't give Latimer the chance to reply. He stood up, turned on his heel and within a few moments Latimer was left alone, staring sightlessly at the blank wall on the other side of the office.

5

Seth Williams, one of the three ex-miners who owned the livery stable, along with their youngest brother, stepped back from the buggy and turned to Latimer.

'She ain't fast but she's nice an' quiet, Sheriff,' he said to Latimer who sat with the reins of the grey in his hand. 'Take you and your lady for a really comfortable ride.'

'Thanks, Seth. Guess it's been a while since I took a buggy ride.'

With a flick of the reins Latimer urged the grey forward and a few minutes later the rig was heading down Main Street for the hotel. He was aware that one or two of the townsfolk shot him puzzled looks as he passed but he pushed any doubts from his mind. Maybe he hadn't been totally honest with Gibbons but he certainly intended to try and gain more information from

Emma Parkes. He hoped a gentle ride out to the lake and the picnic basket stowed behind him would put her in a co-operative mood. He doubted if her claim could be tied in with Kerswell's work but before he tackled the government man he wanted to hear what Emma Parkes had to say.

He brought the buggy to a halt outside the hotel, and saw her emerge from the main door, carrying her document case. That surprised him, but he didn't fool himself that she'd look upon this buggy ride in the same way as he did. He stepped down from the buggy to offer his arm as she came down the steps to the street.

'Good day, ma'am,' he said. 'There's a pretty lake out to the west near the homesteads. Lots of interestin' birds visit this time of the year.'

Preparing to step up to the buggy, she halted suddenly, her hand resting on his arm. 'I wish to go east, Mr Latimer, to see my land.'

'That's impossible ma'am. Armand

and his no-goods could be around.'

She removed her hand from his arm. 'Would you say the Lazy T is a large ranch, Sheriff?'

'Very large, ma'am.'

'Then what are the chances of those men being on or even close to my 160 acres?'

'Very small,' he admitted. 'I just don't want you to risk it.'

She began to turn away. 'Then maybe someone else will take me.'

For the second time in less than four days he had a burning desire to put Emma Parkes over his knee and give her a good spanking. He couldn't argue with her logic. That was what made the situation so damnable. He realized that if he wanted to know more about what was going on and, he had to admit, to enjoy the pleasure of her company for a few hours, he'd have to go along.

'I'll take you to see your claim.'

She placed her hand again on his arm. 'My land,' she corrected sweetly, a smile on her face. 'Shall we go?'

They rode along in the buggy for half an hour or so in companionable silence, enjoying the fair weather. Latimer was content to let the grey have her head, the horse trotting along before falling back to a walk for a while before resuming her trotting. He could think of a hundred questions he'd like to ask Emma Parkes but he thought it wiser to have her open any conversation.

'How long have you been sheriff, Mr Latimer?' Emma Parkes asked, finally breaking the silence.

'Almost ten years,' Latimer said. 'After the war I was working for the Winchester Company and heading for Cheyenne. I stayed off in Beaver for what I thought would be a couple of nights.' He grinned at his memories. 'There was a shooting competition in town which I won, and the mayor offered me the job. The town was having a few troubles back then an' they wanted someone who'd seen army life. I guess what they really meant was someone who'd been shot at before.' He grinned. 'So I took on the badge. Youngest sheriff in the Territory, they told me.'

'Has it always been this . . . ?' Her voice trailed away, as she appeared to be searching for the right word.

'This tough?' Latimer said. 'I've had nine years of a quiet life. But I've been feelin' these last few days I'm back in the army.' He looked up at the stand of cottonwoods to the right of the track they were bowling along. 'We'll be on Lazy T land in ten minutes or so. You sure you want to go ahead?'

'I'm sure.'

He glanced at her, seeing the determined set about her lips. For a moment he wondered what her motives were in pursuing the claim. The idea of Emma Parkes working a homestead was laughable, and the value of the land wouldn't buy one of her silk dresses.

'What brought your father out here those years ago?' Latimer asked.

'He left the army engineers before the war when he was injured in an explosion. He was still young enough to be an eager pioneer, but it didn't work out.' She smiled. 'His good fortune, as his life showed later. He went back East and became a very wealthy man.'

'You've been lucky.'

She nodded. 'I know that.' She looked at him, as if remembering something. 'Is there a Vardon family in the town?'

Latimer shook his head. 'Nobody of that name I recall, nor among the homesteaders. Why d'you ask?'

'The name was mentioned to me, that's all.'

He'd have pursued the topic had he not seen the post on the side of the track that announced that they were now on Lazy T land. 'Don't be alarmed,' he said, as he fished behind him for his gunbelt. 'But I'm gonna rest more easy with it handy.'

He looked around as he buckled on his gunbelt but nothing moved on the wide open landscape of what appeared to be never-ending bunch and buffalo grass. Over to his right was the creek he'd previously identified on the document shown to him by Emma Parkes. On its banks he could see the churned up ground where the Lazy T beef had come down to take the water. Emma Parkes spread out over her lap the document she'd taken from her case and placed a finger on the map.

'We must be close,' she said. 'Northwest from here.'

He tautened the grey's reins to turn her head and the buggy left the track and headed towards where Emma Parkes believed her father's homestead had once stood. Latimer doubted if anything remained after all the many harsh Wyoming winters, but the young woman was determined to reach the actual site and he'd go along. He scanned the horizon again without making it too obvious. He didn't wish to frighten her but he knew he wouldn't rest easily until they were heading back to Beaver.

'Another hundred yards and we should be where the cabin once stood,' she said.

Latimer grinned at the excitement in her voice. She'd obviously been fond of her late father and maybe this was her way of honouring his memory and part of his life. He hauled back on the grey's reins as the young woman half stood up from her seat.

'We're here,' she said triumphantly.

Without waiting for Latimer to assist her, she stepped down to the ground and strode forward, her skirts brushing the grass. Behind her, Latimer again scanned the empty horizon.

'Look at this!'

He turned to see her pointing down to the ground. There appeared to be only grass around her feet but he walked across to her to see what she had found. Barely visible through the grass were several large stones set in a square. 'This must have been the chimney for the cabin my father built,' she said gleefully, as if she'd struck gold.

Latimer's face split in a broad grin. 'I guess you're right, ma'am. Maybe there are other signs 'round here.' He turned to examine the area around the old chimney stones, and stood very still. A group of riders were heading in their direction.

'Ma'am, I want you to walk straight back to the buggy. Don't argue, just do as I say.'

The harshness of his voice caused her to look up at him sharply, and then she turned to look in the direction he was facing. 'Oh, my God,' she said, and broke into a swift walk.

'If they're cowboys we ain't gonna be bothered,' Latimer said, his mind racing. He knew that if they weren't cowboys the buggy could never outrun them. He could make a stand, but if there was shooting the odds were against him and what would happen to the young woman? He followed her, his eyes on the riders. He reached the buggy and swore inwardly as he recognized Armand at the head of the group.

'Why don't we run?' He could detect the fear in her voice.

'They'd catch us in minutes,' he said. 'I ain't sure how this is goin' to pan out. There could be shootin'. I shout 'Down!' an' you get your face in the dirt as fast as you can. It ain't ladylike but you gotta do it. You un'erstand?'

'I understand.' Her face was pale, her eyes on the group of men as they neared the buggy where she and Latimer sat.

'Now you just go along with anythin' I say. Just like you did in my office yesterday,' Latimer said. 'They're no-good gunslingers an' they ain't blessed with too many brains. We gotta chance o' talkin' ourselves outa trouble.'

Again she nodded, instinctively pushing herself closer to Latimer as the five men reined in their horses, with shouts of triumph. Four of them circled the buggy whooping and shouting while Armand urged his horse forward to halt a few feet away from the buggy, a leer on his face.

'You sure make my job a lot easier, Latimer. I reckoned I was gonna have to come into Beaver for you.' He looked straight at Emma Parkes. 'An' you even bring me a mighty pretty present.'

'Save some for me, boss,' shouted one, to the coarse laughter of his companions.

'You're making a big mistake, Armand,' Latimer said.

'Yeah?' Armand snickered, and looked at the other riders. 'You hear what Latimer says? I'm makin' a big mistake!' The four riders yelled with laughter as Armand stared hard at Latimer.

'That tin star ain't worth spit on a rock out here.' Armand drew his sidearm. 'I shoot you as a trespasser on Mr Danton's land. You think anyone's gonna argue with that?'

'If you shoot me you're gonna have to shoot the woman.'

'Now why should I have to do that?'

'Because I shall testify at your trial for murder,' Emma Parkes said, her voice surprisingly firm to Latimer's ears. 'You will hang and I shall be there to watch.'

Armand threw back his head and laughed loudly. 'Got yourself a real feisty lady here, Latimer!' His face hardened, his apparent good humour disappearing in an instant as he looked at Emma Parkes. 'So I'll have to shoot you as well,' he paused, 'after you an' me an' the boys here have a little party, that is.'

'You ain't listenin' to me, Armand,' Latimer said. 'I just said you were makin' a big mistake.'

'You'd say anythin' to save your neck.'

'I'm sayin' you touch even a hair on Miss Parkes's head you're gonna hate yourself until the moment the hangman pulls the lever, an' maybe for a few minutes after that.'

'What the hell you talkin' about?'

'Listen, you ruffian! Have you any notion how wealthy my husband is?' Emma Parkes said sharply. 'Back East he has fifty Pinkerton men guarding his companies. He could hire fifty more if he's so minded.'

Latimer saw the four men exchange glances behind Armand. One of them, wearing a leather waistcoat, pulled up his mouth and shook his head. Latimer snatched at his opportunity.

'You wanna study on what a hundred Pinkerton men could do to the Lazy T?' Latimer said to Armand. 'You wanna guess who'd be first to hang you an' the rest of this bunch? You wanna choose between the Pinkertons or Josh Danton? I've heard the Pinkertons favour a man strangling a while at the end of a rope over havin' his neck broke.'

'This ain't helpin' Ned none,' one of the men said.

Armand swung around in his saddle. 'Shut your mouths you wanna see nightfall.' He swung back to face the buggy. 'You get off this ranch now, Latimer, afore I change my mind. But I'm givin' you a warnin'! You keep Will Danton in a cage an' I'm gonna be ridin' into Beaver, an' you an' me can settle what's between us.' With a cruel jab of his Californian spurs into the side of his mount he pulled round the animal's head and galloped away followed by the four riders.

★ ★ ★

For almost half an hour Latimer and Emma Parkes sat silently as they rolled back in the direction of the town, occupied with their own thoughts. Latimer wasn't fooling himself. He knew he could have died out there, and Emma Parkes would have faced a bad time before they finally killed her. Despite her courage in facing Armand he knew she'd been badly shaken. He decided to keep his mouth shut until she was ready to speak.

The marker came up for the limit of

Lazy T land, and alongside him she sighed heavily, as if releasing the pentup fear that must have been weighing on her since they first saw Armand and his men. He glanced at her alongside him and saw her colour was beginning to reappear.

'I hope you'll forgive me, Mr Latimer,' she said quietly.

He remained silent for a few moments. 'There's nothing to forgive,' he said finally. 'You were fine back there.'

'I almost got you killed,' she said.

'Is your husband really that rich?'

'I have no husband. My eldest brother owns the company. A husband sounded better.'

Her lips curved in a smile, not strong, he noticed, but it was a smile. Latimer's face, too, broke into a smile. Hell, this was some woman alongside him in her fancy skirts and her Boston accent. He'd marvelled at her beauty from the moment he'd first laid his eyes on her, but had also wondered how she would fare in Beaver. Back there with Armand she'd shown true courage, and he admired her for it. He couldn't resist looking directly at her, and saw that she had now regained her composure, her colour now totally returned, and her blue eyes steadily returning his gaze.

'He must have a lot of companies to hire fifty Pinkertons.'

'He does have many companies but I think he has five Pinkertons,' she paused, 'maybe only four.'

Latimer knew his jaw had dropped with total surprise at her words. He threw back his head and laughed loudly. Maybe it was out of sheer relief knowing that for a while back there his fate hung by nothing stronger than a saddle string.

'Ma'am, are all the ladies back in Boston like you?'

A full smile now showed on her face. 'Not many. My brothers consider me wayward.'

'Then you just carry on bein' as wayward as you please — ' Latimer broke off as he saw the rider approaching them fast from the direction of Beaver Creek. 'Now what's young Dexter from the livery got ants in his pants over?'

The rider approached them at a full gallop, hauling back on his reins as he reached a few yards away from where Latimer had halted the buggy, his mount skittering across the grass.

'Ma'am,' Dexter said breathlessly, touching the rim of his battered hat to acknowledge Emma Parkes. 'Sheriff Latimer, Deputy Wilson needs you back in town mighty quick.'

'What's goin' on, Dexter?'

'Mr Turner, the man works for Mr Kerswell, he's been found murdered.'

6

Latimer pushed open the door of his office. Behind his desk sat Harry Wilson who stood up smartly when he saw Latimer. In front of the deputy sat Mrs Dora Mackie, the traveller who'd been invited along with Emma Parkes to join Kerswell's stage. In her hand she held a small blue handkerchief as she attempted to stem the tears that coursed down her plump cheeks.

'Glad you're back, Sheriff. Mrs Mackie's been helpin' me with what happened,' Wilson said. He moved from behind the desk to take up his usual position close to the pot-bellied stove. Latimer crossed to hang up his hat before taking his place behind the desk.

'Afore I ask you any more questions, Mrs Mackie, I need to hear from Mr Wilson.'

She nodded her head, her eyes

blurred with tears, and again mopped at her cheeks. 'I understand, Sheriff.' A tear ran down her face to drop onto the material of the shirt covering her ample bosom. 'He was such a courteous man.'

Latimer looked across at Wilson. 'Tell me what happened.'

'Fred Warner, the boy who helps in the general store, had an errand to run for Mr Epson. He took a short cut down the alleyway back of the livery. He found Turner's body slumped against the wall of the livery. He'd been shot.'

'Any of the townsfolk see or hear anythin'?'

Wilson shook his head. 'Nobody saw anythin'. That maybe ain't too surprisin'.' He frowned. 'Strange thing is nobody heard anythin'.'

Latimer glanced at Mrs Mackie whose head was lowered, her handkerchief clutched in her hand. Latimer's expression told Wilson he wanted to know why she was here.

'Mrs Mackie had been with Mr

Turner only a few minutes before his body was found,' Wilson explained. 'I asked her to come across so I could ask her some questions.'

Latimer nodded, and turned to address the woman. He deliberately kept his voice soft. 'Mrs Mackie, I'm sorry I'm gonna have to ask you maybe the same questions Mr Wilson has asked. When the marshal arrives I'm gonna have to report the full details. So I need to know for myself exactly what happened.'

She raised her head, and nodded. 'I understand, Mr Latimer. I'll do anything to help find the blackguard who killed Mr Turner.'

'Thank you, ma'am. How was it you were with Mr Turner a short time before he was killed.'

'Mr Turner and I had become friendly since I joined Mr Kerswell's stagecoach,' she said. 'He was such a kind and courteous man. Since we arrived in Beaver we'd taken to walking around the town together.' She managed a weak smile.

'Some of the town's ladies thought it rather improper, but I found Mr Turner's company most pleasing.'

Latimer frowned. 'I'm not sure I'm followin' you, ma'am. Were you with Mr Turner when he was killed?'

She shook her head. 'No, he left me at the corner of the alleyway at the back of the livery stable. I walked alone towards the hotel.'

Latimer's frown deepened. 'He didn't walk you back to the hotel?'

'At my request, Sheriff. I had to call at the dry goods store to see Mrs Larkins in order to purchase some clothing of a personal nature.' She looked away from Latimer to gaze through the window. 'I thought it improper for Mr Turner to be present in the store.'

The thought skipped through Latimer's mind that Mrs Mackie's sense of what was proper or improper could have cost Turner his life, although there would have been other times somebody took on Turner. In his line of business not many men grew old. Would a

107

woman born in the West have been so sensitive? How would Emma Parkes have reacted? He pushed the thought away. He'd gain nothing by having thoughts like those.

'I made my purchase and after leaving the store I walked alone to the hotel. I remained in my room alone until Mr Wilson came for me. I didn't see Mr Turner alive after the moment I left him.' Her head went down, and she raised her handkerchief to wipe away the tears that welled up in her eyes.

Latimer got to his feet. 'Thank you for your help, Mrs Mackie. I'm sorry you have lost a friend.'

She stood up, her handkerchief held at the corner of her eye. 'Mr Turner was a true gentleman,' she said sadly. 'I shall miss his company on the journey to Fort Laramie. God rest his soul.'

★　★　★

'Fuller's men have joined those no-goods out at the Lazy T,' Latimer said when he and Harry Wilson were alone. 'I met four of 'em earlier today.' He explained briefly what had happened during his buggy ride with Emma Parkes. 'Fact is, Harry, Fuller's got someone workin' undercover in the town. We have to do somethin' about that.'

'More Volunteers?' Wilson suggested.

'I reckon so.' He smiled grimly. 'This business is sure sortin' out the Volunteers who are steady. You scare up another two an' I'll take a walk across the hotel. Where's Turner's body now?'

'At the undertaker's place.'

'OK, I'll go see Joe Sterne after I've been to the hotel.' Latimer paused, and looked hard at his deputy. 'You still OK with all that's goin' on, Harry?'

Wilson twisted his mouth. 'I reckon I'm gettin' ten years' experience in a few days. But yeah, I'm OK. You learn anythin' more from Miss Parkes?'

'She's a brave gal, I know that.' Latimer shook his head. 'I'm minded to think that her claim ain't connected with Kerswell's work but I'm gonna have a talk with that gentleman. He may be an important feller back east but out here he's involved in a coupla murders.'

After Wilson had left to round up another couple of Volunteers Latimer walked over to the hotel to see Jed Morgan. He'd expected to find Morgan only too keen to please, seeing as he was making plenty of money from his unexpected visitors. So Latimer raised his eyebrows when at first Jed Morgan turned down his request.

'Listen Jed, I ain't arguin' with you,' Latimer said. 'I want Mr Kerswell moved upstairs for his own safety. You'd better move the ladies as well. I'm gonna put a Volunteer in their corridor with a scatter-gun. Anyone tries anythin' an' he'll get a faceful of buckshot.'

'But Jack,' Morgan continued to protest, 'The rooms up there ain't my best. I got one which needs workin' on, an' all sorts of rascals have been sleepin' up there these last days.'

'Then you'd better get the place

cleaned up. I'm gonna be seein' Mr Kerswell in a few minutes.'

Morgan put up a hand, acknowledging defeat. 'Don't know what the town's comin' to, Jack, with shootin's an' men gettin' killed. But OK, I'll do as you want.'

Latimer walked along the corridor to the room Kerswell occupied. He knocked and waited. After a few moments a voice bade him enter and he opened the door to find Kerswell at his writing desk turned towards him.

'Do you have any more news of the terrible business with my secretary?' Kerswell said, rising from his chair to move across to the soft chair in the centre of the room. He gestured to Latimer that he should take the chair opposite.

'Mr Kerswell,' Latimer said, once he was seated, 'you have your own reasons for secrecy an' I respect them. But I know Mr Turner was your bodyguard not your secretary. I've not acquainted you with this before because Turner told me you're a busy man with important work to do.'

Kerswell looked at Latimer for a few seconds before replying. 'Did Turner tell you anything about my work?'

Latimer shook his head. 'He told me he didn't know.'

Kerswell smiled grimly. 'Turner was a good man. I'm here on government business. The President himself has directed that corruption in the Indian Bureau is to be investigated. I've been tasked with investigating land thefts from the Shoshone Indians. They signed their treaty in good faith and moved from their homelands. It don't sit pretty back East for blackguards to have come in and taken the land.'

'You mean folks just came in and stole it?'

'No, Mr Latimer, they were much smarter. They bribed officials in the Indian Department to produce false papers showing ownership and then they moved out here and settled the land.'

'Are you sayin' that Josh Danton's involved?'

Kerswell shook his head. 'No, I can't say that. I have my suspicions but they could be unfounded. Documents to help prove the legal ownership of the Lazy T should have been here when I arrived. Without the telegraph I can't be sure, but I hope a rider has left Fort Laramie and will soon be here with all the papers.'

Latimer thought for a moment. 'Some years ago afore I arrived here homesteaders tried to settle land now claimed by the Lazy T. Danton hired gunslingers to drive them off. Some of them moved to the west of the town, others quit and moved on, or went back east. Could that be part of what you're doin'?'

Kerswell smiled grimly. 'Mr Latimer, if we went after all the men who'd driven off homesteaders we'd be removing all the ranchers from the Territory.' He shook his head. 'No, this is about legal ownership. The final documents should give me the answer to take back East.'

Latimer pursed his lips. 'Some folks are aimin' to stop you doing that, Mr Kerswell. My job is to keep you alive. I've arranged with Jed Morgan that you'll be moved upstairs, an' I'll have a man standing guard in the corridor.'

'I'm most grateful, Sheriff, but I hope the ladies will be moved, too,' Kerswell said. He waved a hand in the direction of his writing desk. 'I do value their presence in the corridor after I've finished my work.'

Latimer remained expressionless. 'I'm sure Jed Morgan will fix that, Mr Kerswell, an' I shall keep you informed of my actions over Mr Turner. Good day, sir.'

Satisfied he'd made the best possible arrangements Latimer left the hotel and spent five minutes with the doctor at his clapboard before crossing the street once more to where Joe Sterne, the town's undertaker and carpenter, had his place near the livery stable. He pushed open the door to see the undertaker behind his desk writing on a long sheet of paper. There was a strong scent of pinewood, and on the floor a few curls of shavings had been trodden into the matting from the workshop behind Sterne.

'I guess you wanna see Turner,' Sterne said, putting down his pen.

'You got him laid out?'

Sterne tapped the sheet of paper in front of him. 'Just finished writing the two lists of his belongings.' He handed one of the papers to Latimer who tucked it into a pocket of his trail jacket. 'Next of kin could turn up demanding I turn over his effects.'

Latimer shook his head. 'That's not gonna happen. Turner was in a dangerous line of work an' his kinfolk musta known. But hold onto 'em until I give you the word.' He looked at the open door behind Sterne.

'You got him out back? I need to see the body.'

Sterne stood up. 'He's on the table. I'll show you.'

The two men went through to the workshop where the scent of pinewood grew even stronger in Latimer's nostrils. The stone floor was littered with wood shavings, and over to the right, pine coffins stood, some with their lids leaning alongside the wall, others only half finished. In the centre of the room Turner was laid out on a wide pinewood table, a white sheet covering from his ankles to his shoulders. From where Latimer stood Turner looked as if he were asleep.

Latimer said. 'You wanna take off the sheet?'

Sterne stripped the sheet from the body. For a moment Latimer stood still, trying to recall the words of the town's reverend. Something about going out of this world as naked as when we came in. He walked around to the other side of the body, and frowned. He could see no evidence of a gunshot wound.

'I was told he'd been shot.'

'He was,' Sterne said. He flicked the sheet and covered the body again. 'The wound's are at the back of his neck. Come 'round here an' I'll turn his head an' you'll see 'em.'

Latimer moved to stand at the end of the table. Sterne reached forward and easily moved the head. Some time would pass before the body began to stiffen. At the back of Turner's head, below the hairline, Latimer could see two round black holes. There were no signs of exit wounds, and he realized the slugs, .22s he guessed, were inside Turner's head. He stepped back, and as he did so he heard Mills call from the outside office.

'Sheriff! Mr Sterne! You folks here?'

'Through here, Doc,' Latimer called, and turned as Mills stepped into the room, carrying his small leather bag. 'Here's the feller I was tellin' you about.'

Mills looked at the body. 'What is it you want me to do?'

'There's a coupla slugs inside him. I wanna take a look at 'em.'

Mills pursed his lips as he saw the

wounds on Turner's neck. 'They in his head?'

''Fraid so.'

'Then I'm gonna have to take a saw to him.' He looked at Sterne. 'That OK with you, Mr Sterne?'

The undertaker shrugged. 'This poor critter ain't gonna feel no pain. Might be more friendly if you do it at night when I ain't here, an' you patch him up after.'

Mills nodded. 'I can do that.' He turned to Latimer. 'I'll come across before supper. I'll let you know as soon as I've dug the slugs out.'

Latimer was about to leave when he remembered a question that Emma Parkes had put to him. 'Doc, you've been in Beaver the longest of us all, I reckon. You ever heard of a Vardon family?'

Mills pulled up his mouth and began to shake his head, and then he snapped his fingers with exasperation. 'Sometimes I think my mind's goin'. There was a Sally Vardon 'round these parts, but that was twenty years ago. There wasn't a Vardon family, I recall. She came to the town alone. She was — ' Mills stopped suddenly as if changing his mind about what he was going to say. 'She left town,' he went on, 'an' was never heard of again. Why d'you ask?'

Latimer shrugged. 'The name came up, that's all. Leave the slugs with Joe. I'll pick 'em up later.'

★ ★ ★

Latimer was back in his office waiting for Harry Wilson to come back with the news that he'd found another couple of Volunteers. Wilkins and Holland would have spread the word that the town was paying their wages but that didn't mean the Volunteers would be rushing forward to help out. Most of the Volunteers were too young to have been in the War, and maybe they were reckoning that handling logs was less dangerous work.

He looked up as the door opened

expecting to see his deputy, and was pleasantly surprised to see Emma Parkes. Since she'd arrived in Beaver he realized that he'd been in her company most days, and though some of those times had been mighty trying, he felt better every time he saw her.

He stood up and gestured to the chair. 'I sure hope you ain't bringin' me more trouble, Miss Emma.' He waited to see if she gave any sign of her objecting to his using her name but her expression remained unchanged.

'I hear you're having us moved upstairs at the hotel,' she said.

'I think you'll be safer,' he said.

'Mr Kerswell will be safer,' she said. 'Nobody is trying to kill me.'

He looked at her hard. 'Who said anyone was tryin' to kill Mr Kerswell?'

Her mouth twitched, and there was a look in her eyes that he couldn't ignore, but she remained silent. 'Armand threatened you,' he pointed out.

'Only because he meant to do you harm and thought I was in the way.'

120

He breathed in deeply. 'I'll tell Jed Morgan you're staying downstairs.'

'I've a better idea,' she said. 'As I've decided to stay for a while I'm looking for a clapboard to rent.'

If Emma Parkes was going to be around for a while that was just fine with him, and, he realized, he could help her out. The clapboard he had in mind was alongside that of the doctor's and she'd be safe enough there.

'Doc Mills has a clapboard he's seekin' to rent out. Old Judge Baker lived there alone until he died a few weeks ago, but he was well looked after by one of the women in the town. There's probably a lot of the judge's stuff left in there but the house should be clean and it would do you fine.'

After Emma Parkes had left, having promised to speak with the doctor, Latimer sat at his desk turning over the recent events in his mind. Before long Josh Danton would appear in town demanding the release of his son. He was surprised Danton hadn't arrived already, and he guessed that the rancher was away from the Lazy T for a while.

Latimer could guess what would happen. Danton would see Gibbons first to warn him that the town would suffer if his son was not released. Beaver didn't rely on the Lazy T for its prosperity. The logging and the saw-mill brought money to the town, but Josh Danton had friends in high places. The threats of business deals collapsing and bad trading conditions could persuade folks to press Gibbons for Will Danton's release.

But if that didn't get his son released Danton had stronger cards to play. The rancher could send in Armand and his men to bust Will Danton out of jail whatever the cost, and there'd be plenty of folks willing to turn a blind eye if it meant peace returning to the town. Latimer had no problem with facing Armand alone but he knew it wouldn't be just the two of them. Armand would bring in as many men as he could. Latimer thought for a moment. Maybe

Armand could be outwitted. The no-good was faster with a gun than with his brains, and a gunfight might be avoided. Latimer got to his feet as the street door opened and Harry Wilson appeared.

'OK, Mr Latimer, another coupla Volunteers have stepped forward. They'll start after noon.'

'I reckon we'll see Danton here tomorrow,' Latimer said. 'I'm gonna have a word with Henry Gibbons. We don't want him makin' promises that I ain't prepared to keep.'

7

Latimer had taken an early breakfast and was studying the list of Turner's effects given to him by Joe Sterne, the undertaker, when Harry Wilson burst through the door.

'Josh Danton's with the Mayor. He's gonna be here mighty soon.'

'OK, we know how we're gonna play this, Harry. We don't give him Miss Parkes's name unless he demands it.'

'We got a problem with that, Sheriff.' Wilson pulled back his lips in an expression of frustration. 'My pa's with him.'

'Your pa! What the hell's he doin' with Danton?'

'Danton must have hired him.' Wilson saw the scowl on Latimer's face. 'He can't refuse to give legal advice, Sheriff, if he's asked.'

'Where's that fast-talkin' lawyer in

fancy clothes that Danton brings up from Fort — ?' Latimer stopped suddenly. 'Hell! I clean forgot 'bout the bridge for a second.'

Wilson was looking through the window into Main Street. 'Three of 'em, Sheriff, comin' this way. The mayor's with Danton and Pa.'

Latimer got to his feet. He didn't want Danton and Gibbons bearing down on him while he sat behind his desk trying to justify the decisions he'd taken. Through the window he saw the shoulders and heads of the three men. Then the door was thrown open, and Danton stormed into the office, his face black with fury. Behind him came Abe Wilson, and finally, scowling with worry, came Henry Gibbons.

Danton didn't bother with greetings. 'I wanna see my son!' he roared.

'My deputy will accompany you, Mr Danton,' Latimer said calmly. He looked across the room. 'Harry, show Mr Danton through to the cages.'

Danton swung on his heel. 'You stay

here, Gibbons. Mr Wilson, you come with me.'

Harry Wilson led his father and Danton through the door to the rear of the office, closing the door when the two had passed through into the passageway.

Gibbons swung on Latimer. 'I warned you! I goddamned warned you this would happen!' He pulled out his spotted handkerchief and mopped furiously at this forehead. 'Danton's threatenin' to block the licences for the mill when they come up next month. You and your high-minded stand are gonna ruin this town.' Gibbons stepped forward, his fists clenched. 'Folks have given their whole lives to build Beaver Creek, an' you're gonna tear it down!'

Before Latimer had chance to reply, the door leading to the cages was thrown open, and Danton burst into the room. 'Will said he didn't do it. That's good enough for me. Why the hell d'you think my son would kill a homesteader's boy?'

'He was tryin' to kill Mr John Kerswell, the boy got in the way.'

'You're outa your mind, Latimer. What evidence you got for that?'

'Someone saw your son shoot young Jenkins.'

'Who's sayin' that?' Danton barked. 'Bring him in here an' let me hear him say that to my face!'

'The witness has identified your son twice.'

Danton snorted. 'I'm tellin' you again, Latimer. I wanna know who this witness is. I gotta legal right.' He looked sideways at Abe Wilson. 'That's true, ain't it?'

Wilson nodded briefly. 'That's correct, Mr Danton.'

Danton swung back to face Latimer. 'So let's hear this feller's name, Sheriff.'

'The witness is a lady.'

Danton's eyes bulged. 'A lady?' he exploded. 'You've got my son in jail on what some damned woman says.' He took a pace closer to Latimer's desk, his eyes bloodshot with rage. 'I wanna hear her name and I wanna see her now.'

Latimer glanced past Danton's shoulder to see Abe Wilson indicate by his expression that Latimer had no choice. For an instant he wondered if he'd be signing Emma Parkes's death warrant by giving her name to Josh Danton. If she were unable to testify at a trial Will Danton would walk from jail a free man. Did he have the right to gamble with her life? Why shouldn't he say to hell with it and release Danton? There'd be no showdown with Armand and his bunch of gunslingers, Gibbons would be happy, and the townsfolk would be free to go about their business.

But how many times over the past nine or ten years had he told the townsfolk that if Beaver was to prosper then the law had to be supported? If he backed down now and gave into demands from Danton he knew he'd have to quit Beaver and make a start somewhere else. Not only that, he'd have to live with the decision for the rest of his life. Harry Wilson would reckon he'd broken his solemn oath. Emma Parkes would return to Boston convinced he was a weak man, and she'd be right.

'I'm still waitin' for an answer, Latimer.'

'Miss Emma Parkes from Boston,' Latimer said.

Danton's jaw dropped with furious disbelief. 'Are you outa your mind? Some damned pilgrim from back East. Get the woman here now!'

Latimer looked across to Harry Wilson. 'Ask Miss Parkes to join us. Tell her it's important.'

Wilson nodded, and Latimer watched him leave the office. His deputy would be smart enough to warn Emma Parkes that she was about to face the most powerful man in the county. He hoped she was strong enough to meet the challenge.

Danton turned to Abe Wilson. 'I wanna word with you outside.'

The two men left the office, leaving Latimer and Gibbons alone. There were a few moments of silence before Gibbons spoke. His voice shook and he was patently making great efforts to keep himself under control.

'Is there any chance this woman will go back on what she saw?'

'I don't know,' Latimer said. 'It's possible. I guess she'll be returning to Boston when the trail reopens. She hasn't a chance of claimin' the land she reckons she owns. I don't see her comin' back West to do justice a favour.'

Gibbons began to speak but was cut off by the door opening and Danton and Abe Wilson coming back into the office. Danton glared at Latimer.

'I guess young Wilson's bringin' the woman with him now.'

A few moments later the door opened and Emma Parkes stepped into the office closely followed by Harry Wilson. He was surprised to see her carrying her document case. She looked directly at Latimer who knew her well enough now to recognize that although she was nervous, she was determined.

'I'm waitin' to have a word with you, young woman!' Danton barked.

Emma Parkes returned his stare unflinching. 'Is that the way you address a lady, Mr Danton? No matter, I shall ignore your poor manners, as I am waiting to have a word with you.'

Whatever Danton was expecting, Latimer realized, the rancher certainly hadn't expected the robust reply from Emma Parkes. He saw Danton hesitate a moment, puzzlement showing in his eyes, before he again showed his anger.

'Your word's put my son in jail, young lady, an' I wanna know what you mean by it.'

'Mr Latimer has put your son in jail, Mr Danton. I merely saw your son shoot that poor boy.'

'Listen to me, my son never killed no-one. He's tol' me that, an' I believe him. But I'm gonna tell you what I've done. Half an hour ago I signed a paper in Abe Wilson's office. My boy walks outa this jail an' the Jenkins family gets a thousand dollars. I know it don't make up for the loss of their boy but you got any notion what a thousand dollars means to poor homesteaders like them folks?'

'A fortune, I imagine,' said Emma Parkes. 'But don't misunderstand me, Mr Dalton. I'm not foolish enough to think I can influence what you men decide. I shall appear if your son comes before a judge. If he does not,' she glanced across at Latimer, 'then what I could say means nothing.'

Danton looked at her for several seconds, as if attempting to read her thoughts, before nodding slowly. 'Maybe I should pay a visit to Boston. Seems folks are movin' along back there.' Maybe Danton meant his words as a compliment but he didn't stop there. 'You can leave us now,' he said.

Later, when he was alone, Latimer decided it was the dismissive tone of Danton's voice when he uttered those last words that fired up Emma Parkes. At the time he saw the colour rush to her face, as Danton, believing that he'd finished his discussion with her, turned his back on her.

'One moment, Mr Danton,' Emma Parkes cut in. 'We have business to discuss. With these gentlemen here, this is a good opportunity.'

Danton turned back to her, an impatient expression crossing his face, as she pulled from her document case the papers Latimer had seen before. Anticipating what Emma Parkes was about to do, Latimer pushed aside his large leather journal, and shifted his inkwell so her papers could be laid flat out on the desk.

Danton looked down at the out-spread sheet of paper. 'What's this?'

Emma Parkes stepped forward. 'It's a map of the area to the east of the town.' She pointed a finger. 'That's the creek.'

'You're talkin' about land belongin' to the Lazy T.' Danton traced with his finger around the red ink close to the blue line marking the creek. 'What's this s'posed to mean?'

'It means a hundred and sixty acres left to me by my father and that are now mine.' She placed another document, bearing red seals, on the desk. 'This is a copy of the ownership document deposited in a Boston bank.'

Blood rushed to Danton's face and a blue vein throbbed at the side of his forehead. 'That was open range homesteaders tried to take twenty years ago. I ran 'em off.' He slammed his fist down on the map. 'Parkes! So that's your game! I remember Parkes. Feller with a big mouth an' a twisted leg. He gave me trouble for over a year.' Danton swung round to face Abe Wilson. 'Tell this woman the law. Parkes had to tend that land for at least five years afore he could claim ownership.'

Abe Wilson turned down his mouth, his discomfort plain. 'That's correct, Miss Parkes. Five years of land improvement is needed.'

'You should keep up with the law, Mr Wilson,' she retorted. 'The government has directed that army service counts

134

towards the five years. My father served four years in the engineers.' She turned back to Danton. 'Under certain conditions I can extend my land to 640 acres. My lawyers are looking into it.'

'Damn your lawyers!' Danton roared. 'You try an' take that land an' you'll never see Boston agin!'

'Make no mistake, Mr Danton, I mean to have my land. Your threats do not frighten me,' she added sharply. 'Ask your ruffian Armand about Pinkerton agents.' She snatched up the two documents and thrust them into her document case. With a brief nod of her head, and a swirl of her skirts, she swept out of the office, brushing past Abe Wilson who had opened the door for her.

There were a few moments of total silence after the door closed before Danton turned on Latimer. 'What's that horseshit 'bout Pinkertons? I'll deal with that damned woman later. She's crazy if she thinks she can drift into town and lay claim to a chunk of the Lazy T. I'm gonna ask you agin, Latimer. You gonna let my boy go?'

Latimer shook his head. 'He'll stay where he is until Judge Hardcastle gets here. He'll decide what happens, not me.'

'You're startin' a war, you know that?' He turned on Gibbons, who was standing in the centre of the office, his face pale. 'You've had your chance Gibbons. You're s'posed to be mayor of this town. I'm tellin' you now, that boy o' mine is gonna be free tomorrow.'

Danton didn't wait for a reply. He turned on his heel and stormed out of the office, slamming the door with such force that it shuddered on its timbers. Abe Wilson expelled air noisily.

'That young woman just made me look a fool,' he said.

Gibbons looked around the room, fury mottling his features. 'Are you all crazy? Abe here's thinkin' of his hurt feelin's. You, young Wilson, are giving support to a sheriff who appears to have lost his mind. You shoulda stuck with your pa, Deputy. Sheriff Latimer's gonna get you killed with him.'

★   ★   ★

After Wilkins had arrived to relieve Holland and Abe Wilson had left with Gibbons, Latimer told Harry Wilson to get his meal. He'd raised a grim smile when Harry turned at the door and, with an attempt at gallows humour, had remarked that he sure hoped it wasn't the meal of a condemned man.

Latimer sat behind his desk trying to guess what was likely to happen the following day. There was every chance that Armand would appear with his gunslingers intent on breaking out Will Danton. With the bridge down, Josh Danton could risk everything settling down before word got to Cheyenne. By then Will Danton could be hundreds of miles away out of the Territory.

If it came to a showdown what were the chances that he and Harry Wilson would survive? He could make a fort out of the jailhouse but that would mean Armand and his no-goods laying siege to them. Gibbons had good reasons for wishing to avoid gunplay on Main Street. Get a reputation like that in the Territory and Beaver would become a target for every no-good for hundreds of miles around. Even were he able to fight off Armand he'd be risking future trouble for the town.

Harry would stand with him, and several of the Volunteers. The Williams brothers from the livery stable didn't lack courage but he was reluctant to ask them to go up against gunslingers. He had no illusions about Armand. The no-good would kill anyone who stood in his way. Latimer suddenly recalled the four men with Armand. Had they joined Armand for a grubstake now Fuller was in jail? Did that show Josh Danton was behind the attempt to kill Kerswell? That would provide a motive for his son trying to bushwhack the government man.

Latimer grunted with exasperation.

So much was happening in the town that it was difficult to decide the truth. This morning he'd have sworn that Emma Parkes was just a modern young woman. But the way she'd held her own against Danton made him think again. He'd read about women, proper ladies, doing all sorts of work back East. There was even a hospital in New York where all the doctors were women. Sure, he knew Emma could be brave, and she was smart, but he remembered Harry Wilson's remarks. Had his deputy detected something about her that he'd missed? Was there a lot more to Emma behind that pretty face?

Latimer threw down his pen with another grunt of frustration. Better he thought about facing Armand than spending his time thinking about a young woman who'd forget him the moment the stage carried her away. His problem would be trying to forget her. That is, he reminded himself, if he was still alive to have such thoughts. He looked up as Harry Wilson came back into the office.

'I'll take over now, Sheriff. The Chinaman's serving a great steak.'

Latimer looked at him thoughtfully. 'Yeah, time I got some grub,' he said. 'But first I gotta job for you.' He explained to his deputy what he needed, and after Harry had made one or two suggestions, Latimer was satisfied that his plan would work.

'I'll go see the Volunteers agin,' Wilson said.

8

The following morning Latimer was taking his breakfast when Henry Gibbons came across to his table. The whole town, including Gibbons, knew that Latimer disliked being interrupted at breakfast and he guessed that the mayor was about to say something that he reckoned couldn't wait a moment longer.

'When you've finished eatin' I think we should have a talk,' he said, looking down at Latimer.

Latimer took a sip of his coffee. 'What more we gotta talk about?'

Gibbons's lips ran over his lips. 'How we gonna get the town outa the mess we're in.'

Latimer shrugged. 'The bridge will be open soon. Kerswell will take off onboard his stage. The marshal will be here to take Will Danton an' Fuller to

Laramie. Don't see too much of a mess 'bout that.'

Gibbons lowered his voice. 'Jack, we have to make a deal. The future of the town rests on it.'

Latimer breathed deeply. He couldn't in all fairness refuse to talk with the mayor. He knew Gibbons was trying to do his best as he saw it.

'I'll be across at the *Clarion* soon as I can.'

'I'm not going to the office. I'll see you at home. Mrs Gibbons is over at the Jenkins homestead.'

'I'll be there,' Latimer said.

'Bring Harry Wilson with you.'

Latimer shook his head. 'Harry's gone over to the homesteads.'

Gibbons nodded. 'I'll see you in an hour.'

Latimer finished his coffee. He was in no hurry that morning. He'd hear what Gibbons had to say, but he'd made up his mind he wouldn't budge from where he stood. Will Danton was going to face a judge, and only the judge would decide if Danton went to trial. If Emma went back east would she return to give evidence? He doubted it, and who could blame her? She had a life back in Boston, and the problems of a small western town like Beaver wouldn't register much in her conscience after she'd taken the railroad from Cheyenne.

Latimer paid the Chinaman and walked across to his office to spend time writing, wondering at the same time what happened to the journals being completed by all the sheriffs of the Territory. Maybe in a hundred years' time some learned man, or even a woman, he supposed, would dust off his own journal in a library and wonder what the hell had caused the quiet town of Beaver Creek to be shaken up in such a short time.

He closed the journal and went out into Main Street and walked along to the mayor's clapboard. He pushed through the white picket fence and went up the path to knock on the door.

Automatically, his hand dropped to his gunbelt buckle. It wasn't done to enter another man's home wearing a sidearm. The door opened and Gibbons stood in front of him, looking as if he'd swallowed a frog.

'Come on in, Jack.'

Latimer stepped into the house and then stood very still, as the barrel of a gun screwed into the nape of his neck hard enough to cut through the skin.

'Just keep on doing what you were about,' said a voice. 'Drop that belt mighty easy.'

Latimer did as he was told, unclasping the large oblong buckle, and with one hand around the belt, allowing his sidearm to rest on the floor. He continued to stand still, knowing that Armand, whose voice he had recognized, would jump at the chance of shooting him down if he made a wrong move.

'I'm sorry, Jack, but it's for the best,' Gibbons managed to stutter.

'Shut your goddamned mouth, Henry,'

Latimer said brusquely. 'You think this is gonna solve anythin'?'

Latimer saw Josh Danton step from a side door and walk into the wide hall of the clapboard. The rancher gestured to Armand and the sidearm was taken away. Latimer ignored the rancher and turned around to face Armand.

'You're out to destroy the lives of decent folks who believe in the law. I'm gonna kill you for that.' Without giving Armand a chance to reply Latimer swung around to face the rancher. 'You got somethin' to say, say it.'

Danton stared hard at him for a few seconds. 'I gave you a chance to release my son. You refused to take it. Now folks tell me you're going courtin' with that fancy woman from Boston. She lyin' for you, sayin' she saw my son shoot that boy, is that it?'

'Miss Parkes is not a liar.'

'I ain't got time to argue. I'm gonna ask you one more time. You gonna let my boy free?'

Latimer drew in a deep breath. 'Your

son will face a judge for what he's done.'

Danton must have given a sign. Latimer's knees buckled as the barrel of Armand's gun hit him on the side of his head. He pitched forward, seeing among clouds of blackness a broad red streak, and for a moment or two he lost consciousness. As the darkness cleared from his mind the barrel of Armand's gun pressed hard against the side of his head. Latimer's mouth went dry as he heard the metallic click of the gun being cocked.

'You said no shooting,' Gibbons yelped.

'Shut your mouth, Gibbons,' Danton rasped, 'afore I have Armand shut it for you.'

The rancher bent down to speak in Latimer's ear. 'We're gonna take my boy outa that jail. We gotta kill that deputy of yourn, we'll do it.'

'Wilson is outa town at the homesteads,' Gibbons said quickly.

Danton nudged Latimer with his

boot. 'That right?'

Latimer, his face against the floor, managed to speak. 'Yes.'

'OK, where are the keys to the cages?'

Latimer remained silent, and Dalton shifted to place his boot on the back of Latimer's neck. 'I ain't gonna ask you agin. Where are the keys?'

'For Christ's sake, Jack! Tell him!' Gibbons spluttered.

'Third drawer down in my desk.'

Armand uncocked his sidearm. 'OK, boss,' he said to Dalton. 'This shouldn't take long.'

Latimer heard the door close behind him, and raised his head to see Dalton drawing his own sidearm. His head was still painful from the blow he'd suffered from Armand's gun but his mind was beginning to work again and he had to do some quick thinking.

'You can get on your feet, Latimer,' Dalton barked. 'Just be goddamned thankful you're alive. But don't you ever put your damned nose into my affairs agin, or I'll have you put on Boot Hill. I got unfinished business in this town an' you'd better keep outa my way.'

For a second, as he scrambled to his feet, Latimer toyed with the notion of challenging Dalton about the presence of John Kerswell but decided he'd be a fool to rile the rancher ever further. As he turned over in his mind his next move the door burst open. Armand stood at the threshold, his arm extended, his gun cocked.

'Where's my son?' Dalton shouted.

'He ain't there! We've been fooled. Nobody's there. The jailhouse is empty.' Armand pulled back his lips to show tobacco stained teeth. 'You want me to kill him now?'

'There's to be no killing in this house!' Gibbons shouted.

'He's *my* son!' Dalton roared. 'If anyone's gonna kill him, it's gonna be *me*.' His sidearm came up to aim at Latimer's chest. 'You sonovabitch! Say your prayers. You're gonna die!'

'You shoot me an' you kill your son,' Latimer said quickly.

Dalton's gun wavered an inch. 'What the hell you mean by that?'

'Harry Wilson ain't at the homesteads. He's in a place you'll not find in time. He's got his orders. I get killed, he's gonna shoot your son, and claim he was trying to escape.'

'Wilson knows the law. He wouldn't do that,' Dalton barked, but his voice betrayed his doubts.

'Deputy Wilson would carry out any order the sheriff gave him,' said Henry Gibbons quickly. Latimer looked across at the mayor. His face was pale, and his hands were trembling but he was looking across to Danton with a suggestion of his usual bearing. 'Wilson is extremely loyal to Sheriff Latimer.'

'He's bluffin', boss. Don't fall for it,' Armand snarled.

'Shut your mouth, Armand,' Danton said. He lowered his gun, and looked at Latimer. 'Nobody's ever said you ain't got brains. But brains ain't gonna keep you alive when you're faced with a whole pack o' guns. I'll know when you bring Will back to the cage. An' my men will be comin' for him.'

He slipped his sidearm into its holster, and without looking at any of the others brushed past Latimer and through the door to the street, closely followed by Armand. The door slammed shut behind them.

Latimer, the sweat running down his back, soaking his shirt, slumped down on the nearest chair. Opposite him, Gibbons did the same.

'What the hell were you tryin' to achieve, Henry?' Latimer said after a moment's silence.

Gibbons bowed his head, his voice muffled. 'They told me Josh Danton wanted to come in and talk, that's all. I had no idea Armand was going to be here.' He raised his head. 'Would Harry Wilson really have killed Will Danton?'

Latimer shook his head. 'Not a chance.' He managed to raise a grin. 'He'd have reported me to the marshal if I'd said such a thing.' He looked at the mayor, whose head was still down, his hand to his brow. 'You said the right words at the right time, Henry. I thank you for it.'

Gibbons raised his head quickly. 'You thankin' me when I almost got you killed? I must have been outa my mind.' Gibbons screwed up his eyes. 'Maybe Beaver needs a new mayor.'

Latimer got to his feet. 'We're gonna get through this together, Henry. The town needs you. We just gotta stand steady. Now I got work to do.'

★ ★ ★

Captain Bracken of the Volunteers puffed on his pipe and sent clouds of smoke swirling to the ceiling of his parlour. His bushy grey eyebrows were pulled together in an expression of amazement and he leaned forward as if to make sure he'd heard Latimer correctly.

'Say that agin. You wanna use the cannon from the square?'

'You heard right, Walter. I got Will Danton an' Fuller stashed away in Jake Palmer's cabin. Harry Wilson's gotta coupla Volunteers with him but he can't last there for more than a day. Danton's gonna learn damned quick his son is back in the cage an' he'll send in his gunslingers to bust him out. I wanna use the cannon to stop 'em.'

'Jack, that cannon hasn't been fired since the War. We got it from the fort for ceremonies, that's all. You try an' use it, an' you're gonna kill yourself an' any man standin' close.'

Latimer nodded. 'I know that, but I gotta stop Armand an' his men from even gettin' into town. I can use that cannon to stop 'em, Walter, but I need your word afore I can move it from the square.'

More smoke swirled from Bracken's corncob towards the ceiling above him. 'You ain't gettin' my word until I've heard how you're plannin' to use it. I ain't gonna be responsible for gettin' men killed.'

152

'You got a pencil and paper?'

'Sure, right handy.' Bracken stretched down to the box beside his chair and pulled out a block of rough yellow paper and a pencil. He leaned forward and handed them to Latimer.

'OK, this is what I'm gonna do.' Latimer made a few pencil strokes on the paper. 'This is the high ground to the east of the town. Armand an' his men have to come in that way.'

He turned the paper around so Bracken could see what he was drawing and spent the next ten minutes explaining his plans, adding that he had to call at the livery stable before he could be sure he'd thought of everything. When he'd finished drawing the last lines on the paper he looked up at Bracken, and was relieved to see a slow smile forming on the old soldier's face.

'Gotta hand it to you, Jack. If it works, it's mighty clever.' Bracken eyes twinkled behind his spectacles and he blew smoke through his grey whiskers. 'But what happens if it don't?'

'Then Harry an' me ride like hell an' face 'em on Main Street afore they reach the jailhouse. I gotta coupla Volunteers willin' to stand with us.'

Bracken nodded. 'Sure hope it don't come to that.'

Twenty minutes later Latimer pushed through the side doors of the livery, hoping to find three of the four brothers. As he walked past the stalls, several of the horses stamped their hoofs. One animal thrust his head forward and attempted to bite Latimer's arm prompting the sheriff to jump aside and rap the animal smartly on his nose with his hat.

'That critter's as ornery as a mule,' a voice called.

Latimer looked to the end of the barn and saw Dexter, the youngest of the four brothers, forking hay from a pile on the ground to a wooden platform above his head.

'Good day, Sheriff. What can I do for you?'

'Your brothers here, Dexter?'

'Sure, they're all workin' out back. Hold on, I'll go get 'em.'

A few minutes later, the three ex-miners came through the door at the end. All three looked hot and dusty, and two of them were carrying long-handled forks.

Seth, the eldest, stepped forward. 'You wanna see us, Mr Latimer?'

'Howdy, Seth,' Latimer said. 'I need a favour.'

Seth held up his hand. 'We'd still be chokin' on dust if you hadn't spoke up for us with the mayor, Mr Latimer. You name it an' if we can do it, we're your men.'

'There's no obligation here, Seth,' Latimer said. 'An' I mean that. You wait to hear what I'm goin' to ask afore you answer.' He reached out for the forks being held by one of the brothers. 'I'll use this an' show you what I mean.' He turned the tines of the fork so he could use one to scratch lines in the soil of the livery floor.

'East o' the town we got the creek

here.' He drew a line in the soil. 'Movin' towards town we got this big stand o' cottonwoods.' He drew a diagonal line and then a circle. 'This ring here is the high ground.' He looked at the three older men while Dexter moved in closer for a better look. 'You followin' me so far?'

All four nodded their heads.

'Tomorrow, I guess 'round noon, Lazy T gunslingers are gonna be ridin' past here heading for the jailhouse. They're aimin' to bust out Will Danton.'

'But you said Danton killed the Jenkins boy,' Seth said quietly.

Latimer nodded. 'He did, Seth. You can take my word. Me and Harry Wilson have gotta stop those gunslingers, an' I need your help.'

'We ain't the fastest with our sidearms, Mr Latimer, but we'll stand with you.'

Latimer looked at each of the men. 'You're all good men, an' I thank you for it, but I gotta better idea than you standin' with guns.'

He took up the fork again and began to draw lines in the soil, explaining what he intended the following day. When he had finished, the men again looked at each other, exchanging nods of agreement. Seth turned back to face Latimer.

'Three of us did work like that every day for ten years. But if those no-goods are comin' in afore noon we'd better get started rightaways.' He turned to the youngest of the brothers. 'You're gonna be part o' this, Dexter. Mr Latimer's gonna need help with that cannon. Use the percheron if you get any trouble.'

9

Shortly before daybreak, half an hour before the town began to stir, Harry Wilson and two of the Volunteers rode along Main Street with their two prisoners. Latimer stood on the board-walk outside his office, a scatter-gun in his hands. He watched as Wilson and the Volunteers dismounted and freed the ropes from around their prisoners. Ten minutes later both Fuller and Danton were back behind bars as a fresh Volunteer arrived to take up his position before the cages.

An hour later Latimer gathered the men around the cannon in the town's square. The few men and women of the town who were already about their business stared with open curiosity at what the men were about. Latimer glanced across at Captain Bracken who had insisted on being present. 'You need an artillery man 'round when you move a cannon,' he'd told Latimer through clouds of blue smoke.

'OK, Dexter,' Latimer called. 'Walk the horse forward, see how she moves.'

Dexter, astride the huge percheron, urged the animal forward with a clicking of his tongue. There came a screeching of metal as the cannon moved from the stone blocks and fell the three inches to the ground with a judder that Latimer felt in the soles of his boots.

'Sheriff, the wheels didn't turn an inch!' Harry Wilson shouted.

Puffs of smoke from his pipe were sent shooting above Bracken's blue cap. 'You're gonna need another bucket o' grease to get that old gal movin',' he called. 'An' I reckon you're gonna need another animal or Dupont's gonna be eatin' that damned horse afore he's ridin' it agin.'

Dexter slid from the percheron's broad back. 'I'll go get the English shire,' he told Latimer. 'We get the wheels movin' an' two horses should be fine.'

'You lookin' for another hand, Jack?'

Latimer turned to see Luke Bartram, owner of the saloon, standing before him in the oldest clothes Latimer had ever seen the saloon owner wearing.

'What the hell you doin' here, Luke?'

'Woke early, an' saw what was goin' on.' Bartram shrugged. 'Reckoned I could do somethin' to help.'

'Luke, I'm mighty grateful. A bucket of grease is what I need now.'

Bartram nodded. 'I'll be back pronto.'

Five minutes later he'd returned, and without any prompting from Latimer set about working on the axles of the wheels that hadn't seen grease for more time than Latimer cared to think about. But by the time Dexter had harnessed the English shire alongside the percheron, Latimer was satisfied they had a good chance of moving the old cannon.

He looked across at Captain Bracken. 'We're ready, I reckon.'

Bracken took the pipe from his

mouth and rubbed his hand across his grey whiskers. 'Go ahead, Jack, and God speed. I damned well wish I was comin' with you.'

Latimer held up his hand. 'You're needed here, Cap'n.' He touched the brim of his hat. 'We'll have a whiskey on this some time.' He turned and called to Harry, who was riding a few yards ahead of Dexter.

'OK, forward ho!'

Wilson moved his horse forward in a walk and Dexter, now mounted on the shire, kicked the animal's sides, urging the two great horses forward as Latimer stared hard at the wheels of the cannon carriage. A pleased grin showed on his face, as he saw the wheels begin to move. The extra grease had done its job, the wheels turning smoothly with no more noise than the rumbling sound of the heavy load being shifted across the hardpack of Main Street.

Latimer mounted his roan, bringing around the animal's head to follow the cannon, giving a cheerful wave in the direction of the two small boys in britches and long woollen stockings as they ran along the boardwalk keeping pace with the procession as it headed out of town. Latimer ignored the puzzled shouts of the townsfolk enquiring what they were about. If he'd told them their destination was the high ground to the east of the town overlooking the trail they'd have thought him crazy.

★ ★ ★

Without Dexter being with them to handle the huge horses Latimer realized they would never have got the cannon up to where it now stood proud on the ridge, easily seen by any rider on the lower ground. The slope up to the ridge had been steeper than Latimer had anticipated and Dexter had had his work cut out driving the horses up the incline hauling the heavy cannon behind them.

'You reckon we're ever gonna get this

back to town?' Harry said, sitting on the ground, his back against a thin cottonwood, breathing deeply.

'I ain't gonna think about it,' Latimer said. 'I'm just damned pleased we've got this far.'

He looked up at the sky, calculating they had about an hour before noon. Somebody in the town, he knew, would have been paid to alert Danton as soon as his son was known to be back in the cage. The earliest Armand and his men could make a move would be noon. That was plenty of time to get a fire going, and collect some wood which they could dampen down with the water they were carrying if it proved too dry.

'We got one problem with this,' Latimer said. 'A cannon shell comin' over your head makes a hell of a noise. I'm gamblin' that in the noise and stuff nobody's gonna think o' that.' He looked at Harry. 'We're gonna have to be ready to hightail it back to Main Street if this doesn't work.'

He turned around to Dexter who'd stepped forward as if he was about to say something. 'Don't even let that notion cross your mind, Dexter. If we have to quit here, you're to stay. I'm givin' you an order, you un'erstand what that means?'

A crestfallen Dexter nodded. 'I un'erstand, Sheriff.'

Latimer crossed to the cannon where he'd rested his old army spyglass. He'd carried it for nigh on fourteen years and though the brass was badly dented in places the glasses were still good. He raised it to his eye to take another look at the thick stand of cottonwoods on the other side of the trail. Nothing moved, not even a branch seemed to quiver in the warm late morning air. With a small turn of the barrel he altered the focus and shifted his view to inspect the trail running alongside the cotton-woods. He could see nothing unusual and he nodded, satisfied.

'Bring up that pole, Dexter.'

From the saddle-bag he'd taken off

his roan, Latimer pulled out a square of bright red material. Using a couple of old saddle strings he lashed the material to the end of the long pole Dexter held in front of him.

'OK, we're gonna use this to signal Seth,' he said. 'Armand's gonna see the cannon and the flag, and assume we're giving him a warning signal. The men with him ain't soldiers, they're no-good cowardly gunslingers, an' they're gonna run.'

'An' if they don't?' Harrry asked.

'Then I'm relyin' on you to shoot 'em down if I give the order.' Latimer stared hard at his deputy. 'But I ain't lookin' for a bloodbath here. We represent the good folks of Beaver, an' our job is to protect them with as little gunfightin' and killin' as possible.'

He looked at Wilson and Dexter in turn. 'OK, we all know what we gotta do. Let's get on with it.'

Less than an hour later they were ready. Dexter was standing by with the flagpole, Harry Wilson had a small fire burning brightly behind the ridge and near to hand a heap of damp wood and an old horse blanket. Latimer stood alongside the cannon, his spyglass to his eye.

'Here they come,' he shouted, seeing the bunch of riders coming from the north-east, the horses loping along at a steady pace. He reckoned there were ten of them, closely bunched, with Armand in the lead. If they weren't stopped and got to shooting their way down Main Street he and Harry would have a tough fight on their hands.

'Dexter, show Seth the flag,' he ordered.

Dexter ran forward, carrying the pole, to stand alongside the cannon at the edge of the ridge. Holding up the pole he waved it in great sweeps from left to right as a soldier might do when sending a semaphore signal.

'Seth knows he's to wait for the second signal,' Latimer said.

He turned to his deputy. 'You ready to go, Harry?'

Wilson showed a grim smile. 'Ready as a plains Indian with his smoke.'

'Fine, both of you stand by for my word.'

Latimer again raised his spyglass to his eye. Armand and his men were fast approaching the dense stand of cotton-woods where they would be in the range of a cannon. He knew he had to get the timing just right. Too early, and Armand might work out what was going on. Too late, and the riders would be past the cottonwoods and heading for Beaver.

'Dexter, the flag!' Latimer shouted. 'Harry, make smoke!'

Through his spyglass he saw Armand turn his head to look in the direction of the ridge on which they were standing. The group of riders made another fifty yards. Where the hell was Seth? An instant later two of the riders closest to the cottonwoods were blown out of their saddles as the ground erupted beneath them in a huge explosion.

In the still air, Latimer could just

hear the men's shouts and the whinnying of the horses as the heads of their mounts were pulled around by riders frantic to discover what was happening to them. Latimer could see Armand, riding in circles, waving his free hand, shouting, attempting to rally his men.

'Flag! Smoke!' Latimer ordered again.

A few seconds later, as the group of riders had regained control of their mounts and begun again to form up into an orderly group, another explosion tore up the ground. Stones and dirt were sent flying high in the air, causing the men to mill around again, their horses crashing into each other. Latimer saw two of the men pointing in the direction of the ridge.

'Flag! Smoke!'

The third explosion came almost instantaneously with Dexter's waving of the flag and the supposed smoke from the cannon being sent up from Harry Wilson's fire. Hardly three seconds had passed for the buried fuse to burn through and Latimer hoped the ex-miners hadn't got too close to the edge of the stand of cottonwoods.

'They're turning back!' Latimer shouted, his spyglass to his eye. The whole bunch of riders save for Armand had turned back to the north-east, spurring their mounts into a gallop. For a few moments Latimer could see Armand looking in direction of the high ground.

'Sheriff!'

Latimer turned to see Harry Wilson on one knee, his Winchester at his shoulder. 'Give me the word. I've got Armand in my sights.'

For a second Latimer hesitated. 'No, let him go. Two men are dead already. Anyways,' he added, 'sometime soon I'm gonna kill that sonovabitch myself.'

★ ★ ★

Three hours later they were back in the town square, a crowd of townsfolk cheering as Latimer, Wilson, and Dexter, assisted by Seth Williams and his two brothers, heaved the cannon back onto its blocks.

'Jack, that cannon's got more history now,' Captain Bracken had said when they'd returned to the town. Bracken had appeared to be so pleased with Latimer's account of the day's events that he'd forgotten to light his pipe. Instead, he chortled loudly and slapped Latimer on the back.

'Those no-goods gonna think twice afore they come into town agin.'

At the time Latimer had agreed with the old soldier, but as he'd again thanked the ex-miners and young Dexter for their help that day, he'd reminded himself that Danton and Armand wouldn't give up easily. They'd be back, and the next time they'd be more wary. Now, with Wilson mounted alongside him, they walked their horses down Main Street. Wilson nodded in the direction of the sheriff's office.

'I reckon you got a visitor, Mr Latimer.' Wilson grinned. 'Gettin' used to callin' on you, I reckon,' he added.

'Now why don't you go get yourself a

beer, Mr Wilson,' Latimer said. 'An' that'll save me from dumpin' you in that horse dung over there.'

Wilson threw back his head and laughed, urging his horse into a trot in the direction of the saloon. 'Reckon I'll just do that, Sheriff. I'll be back in an hour.' He turned, his grin widening, as he moved away. 'Just so's you know, that is!'

A broad smile on his face, Latimer walked his roan the last few yards to the hitching rail outside his office. He stepped easily to the ground looking up to the boardwalk where Emma Parkes stood outside his office door. He flicked a finger at the brim of his hat as he went up the steps.

'Howdy, Miss Emma. What brings you here? Though I'm bound to say,' he added quickly, 'I'm mighty pleased always to see you.'

A little colour came to her cheeks as she bowed her head briefly to acknowledge the compliment. 'Why, thank you, Mr Latimer,' she said, a smile on her face. But then she became serious. 'I need to speak with you.'

'Sure, ma'am. Come on through.'

He pushed open the door and stood back to allow her to enter. As she settled in the chair in front of his desk he hung up his hat and moved over to the stove. Even in the better weather he and Harry kept the fire burning low so that the coffee kept warm. He took down a tin mug, he hesitated, and turned towards her. 'I'd offer you coffee, Miss Emma, but I've no proper cups for you, an' cream an' sugar we don't keep.'

She turned around in her chair and looked up directly at him. 'I'm sure what you have there will be fine, Mr Latimer.'

'That's good,' he said.

He looked at the row of half a dozen mugs, took one down, rejected it, and settled on one he knew Harry had only recently added to the pegs. He poured the coffee and took the mugs across to the desk, putting one close to her chair.

Then he took his seat, and looked at her expectantly.

'The whole town is talking about what you and Mr Wilson did today,' she said.

'We could have done nothin' without Seth and his brothers. You said you wanted to talk.'

She leaned forward and took a sip of the coffee, appearing to consider what she was about to say. She put down the mug and looked directly at Latimer across the desk.

'I'll say I made a mistake about seeing the shooting, if that's what you wish,' she said quickly, as if reluctant to put into words what she was thinking.

He looked at her for several moments before speaking. 'An' why would I want you to do that?'

'I understand now that Josh Danton will do anything to free his son, whatever the cost to you and this town. If that ruffian Armand succeeds in killing you and Mr Wilson, I believe he'll go on to kill Mr Kerswell. At least three good men could die. Others may be killed if it comes to a fight.' Her lips tightened. 'All because of something I saw.'

Latimer took a sip of his coffee, giving himself time to think. 'Miss Emma, me an' Mr Wilson ain't that easy to kill,' he said finally. 'An' while Harry an' me are on our feet, Mr Kerswell's gonna get back east with what he knows. But let's get something clear. Sure, your word is valuable, but much more important is upholding the law. If we don't uphold the law in the Territory, or anywhere in this great country of ourn for that matter, we'll have failed. A boy was shot dead in Beaver when he was about to start out on what could have been a fine life here in the West. As long as I'm alive, I'll see Will Danton goes before a judge. If I'm not around, then Harry Wilson will see to it.' He stopped suddenly, and shrugged his shoulders, a wry smile on his face. 'Sorry, Miss Emma. Guess I'm soundin' a mite preachy.'

Her blue eyes looked straight at him. 'You have said what I thought you would say,' she said. She looked out of the window for a moment before looking back at him. 'I have the clapboard from Doctor Mills. The judge's effects are still around but I can manage.'

Latimer grinned. 'I can't see you scrubbin' floors.'

'I could if I had to, but Widow Winslow will be looking after me. I hear she's a good cook and a good woman.'

'I know her youngest daughter better,' Latimer said. 'Prettiest gal in town.'

Emma blinked a couple of times. 'Oh!'

'She's six years old next month, little Maisie.' Latimer grinned, remembering. 'I gave her candy last year. She'll be after my hide if I forget her special day.'

Emma Parkes's eyes sparkled. 'As tomorrow is my first proper day in the clapboard,' she said, 'Mrs Winslow has promised to make a special supper. I'd like you to join me.'

Latimer hesitated. 'Miss Emma, I ain't after spoilin' your first party. But these are tricky times. You oughtta know there's folks in town who think I should let Will Danton go. They wouldn't care for my company 'round your table.'

'You misunderstand me, Mr Latimer. You'll be my only guest. Mrs Winslow will, of course, be in the house. Do say you'll be there.'

He managed to control his expression. A regiment of Johnny Rebs wouldn't keep me away, he was tempted to say. But he thought too much of her to accept the invitation. Maybe folks did this sort of thing back in Boston but in Beaver Creek it would never do. The smart ladies of the town would probably swoon when they got to hear of it. He wondered if Emma knew how much she was risking her reputation.

'The smart ladies of Beaver — ' he began, unsure of what to say.

'They'll consider me no better than the women in the saloon,' Emma said crisply. 'I'm aware of that. In Boston, Mr Latimer, the opinions of ladies in Wyoming are unlikely to concern me.'

Latimer bowed his head, in a courteous manner that he hadn't employed since his days in the army. 'I'd be delighted to join you, Miss Emma.'

After she'd left, he sat behind his desk, turning over in his mind the day's events. One moment he was outwitting no-good gunslingers, the next moment he was accepting an invitation to supper with a Boston lady.

'What the hell's tomorrow gonna bring?' Latimer said aloud, addressing the empty office.

10

Soon after daybreak Latimer checked on his two prisoners, exchanged a few words with Wilkins, who'd taken over from Holland in the corridor to the cages, and he was back at his desk drinking his morning coffee when a worried-looking Jed Morgan entered his office.

'Sheriff, we had a heap o' trouble last night at the hotel,' Morgan said.

Latimer frowned. 'Why wasn't I called?'

'Mr Kerswell said there was no need, seein' as you got lots to worry 'bout. He could handle it, he said.'

'Kerswell's gonna get hisself killed talkin' like that,' Latimer said briskly. 'Sit down, Jed. You want some coffee?'

Morgan sat down, but shook his head. 'I took my coffee five minutes ago.'

'So tell me what went on.'

'Some no-good tried to kill Mr Kerswell. First any of us knew somethin' was up was when Mrs Mackie began to scream the place down.' His mouth twisted. 'An' hell! Can she scream!'

'How did she come into this?'

'After supper last night she an' Mr Kerswell were talkin'. He was having trouble with his work, reckonin' there was too much noise in his room from the saloon when he liked to do his writing and stuff. Mrs Mackie offered to change rooms with him, saying the noise wouldn't trouble her. After some talkin' between 'em, they agreed to give it a try. They weren't sure how it was goin' to work out so they decided not to tell anyone.'

'So what happened?'

''Bout a coupla hours after midnight, Mrs Mackie came awake to find a man in her room. She screamed, an' kept on screamin'. Woke up the whole damned hotel. Folks were runnin' 'round in their nightcaps askin' what the hell was goin' on.'

'The man got away?'

Morgan nodded. 'Mrs Mackie locks her door at night. By the time the Volunteer got into the room, the man had vanished through the window.'

'An' that was the room Mr Kerswell had been using?'

'That's it, Sheriff'

'How's Mrs Mackie?'

'She's taken a little soup, and is out of her bed. But she's shaken an' stayin' in her room today, she says.'

Latimer stood up. 'You go ahead, an' let her know I'm comin' to see her. She might have recognized the no-good. I'll be 'cross there in ten minutes.'

After Morgan had left and Latimer was reaching for his hat Harry Wilson came into the office. 'I've just heard 'bout last night at the hotel.'

Latimer grunted. 'I'm told Kerswell likes his liquor. Had he been in his own room, he'd be a dead man. Fuller's man got rid of Turner, now he's after the big prize. An' how the hell we gonna smoke him out?' Latimer pulled his hat lower over his eyes. 'I'm just hopin' Mrs Mackie can help. There was a moon last night an' there's always a chance she got a sightin' of him. I'm gonna ask her after I've had a word with Joe Sterne.'

Five minutes later Latimer stepped into the pine-scented funeral parlour where Sterne was hanging up his black coat on a large wooden peg. The undertaker turned to greet him.

'Just planted Turner on the hill. Mr Kerswell turned out with me an' the Reverend but I heard Mrs Mackie is unwell. Glad you came across. I got those slugs Doc Mills dug outa Turner.' Crossing to his desk, Sterne opened a drawer and took out the slugs which he handed across to Latimer. 'Don't see many .22s 'round these parts. Gambler's weapon, I reckon, or maybe a woman's.'

Latimer carefully stowed the two slugs away in an inside pocket of his trail coat before holding up the list of Turner's effects that the undertaker had handed over on his previous visit.

'Joe, don't take what I'm gonna say the wrong way, it's a question I gotta ask you.'

'Fire away, Jack.'

'Are you sure everything you took off Turner is on this list?'

Sterne flushed red. 'Just what the hell are you sayin'?'

'Now take it easy, Joe. I'm just checkin' on somethin'. We been doin' business together for nigh on ten years an' I reckon we're friends. I'm just askin' a question, that's all.'

Sterne drew in a large breath. 'Yeah, no reason for me to blow my top with you. But it's the curse of my profession, folks sayin' we rob the dead. Makes me real mad. Take my word, Jack. Everythin's there.'

'I never thought otherwise, Joe. Had to ask you, that's all.'

Sterne frowned. 'How long those folks gonna be upstairs at Jed Morgan's place?' He picked up a sheet of paper from his table and thrust it at Latimer. 'Just take a look at that. I got work to do in them rooms, an' my boy's walkin' 'round with his tools askin' when he can get to it.'

Latimer glanced down at the list. He saw there were several jobs outstanding at the hotel. 'Soon as the bridge is open, the folks will be gone.' Latimer had a mental flash of Emma Parkes and realized she, too, would be leaving. 'I'll tell you as soon as I know, Joe.'

Outside Sterne's place Latimer halted on the boardwalk a few moments to stare hard along Main Street towards the trail along which Armand and his men had ridden the day before. Some place beyond the curve of the trail Latimer knew a couple of Volunteers were keeping watch. At the first signs of Armand and his riders reappearing they'd been ordered to hightail back into town and alert Latimer.

He walked along the boardwalk and turned into the hotel, stepping aside to avoid the two men carrying large boxes marked with the initials 'EP', and guessed they were Emma's effects being shifted to Judge Baker's old place. He saw Jed Morgan standing behind the reception desk with his clerk. Morgan turned as Latimer reached the desk.

'Mrs Mackie is in Number Three, Sheriff. She's expecting you.'

'Thanks Jed.' He put his hand on the butt of his sidearm. 'The Colt OK?'

'Sure.'

Latimer hadn't expected for a moment that Morgan would object but as long as he'd been sheriff and needed to enter the hotel he'd always checked his sidearm with Morgan. The hotel's owner, he supposed, knew that he couldn't refuse, but it was a little courtesy that went a long way at election time. He went up the stairs, checking the room numbers until he found Mrs Mackie's room. He knocked softly.

'Sheriff Latimer, ma'am,' he called.

There was a short delay, and then Dora Mackie opened the door. She was pale, but appeared to be composed, and stood back to allow him to enter.

'I hope you're feelin' better, ma'am,' Latimer said, as she gestured that he should take a seat. She lowered herself carefully into the soft chair on the other side of the room.

'Thank you, Mr Latimer. I confess it was a frightening experience. I'm just pleased that Mr Kerswell is unharmed.'

'Did you see the man?'

'I saw him clearly for a few seconds. The light from the moon caught his face before he took to his heels.' She pointed to the window that overlooked the side wall of the saloon. 'I'm a light sleeper, Mr Latimer. The softest noise is enough to wake me.'

'You were most fortunate, Mrs Mackie. Can you describe the man?'

She nodded. 'He wasn't a tall man, but he was heavily built.' She frowned as if trying to recall a mental picture of the man. 'His face was narrow,' she said. 'He had a thin nose, and I think he had big ears.'

Latimer smiled encouragingly. 'That's very good, Mrs Mackie.'

'The moonlight fell on his face as he stood in the middle of the room. He had his hand raised, holding a large knife.' Dora Mackie shuddered, and touched her eye with a lilac-coloured handkerchief.

Latimer stood up and walked across to the window and peered through the glass. A strong and agile man with a plank of wood would have no difficulty in reaching the small balcony around the upper floor of the hotel. He turned back to Mrs Mackie.

'If the man is in town I'm sure I'll find him now after your help. You were very brave.'

She dabbed at the corner of her eye. 'I can't help thinking what would have happened to dear Mr Kerswell if we hadn't changed rooms.'

'Quite so, ma'am.'

He went back down the stairs and stepped into the centre of Main Street, turning around to stare up at the balconies of both the hotel and the saloon. Then he crossed the street to climb the steps and push through the batwing doors of the saloon. As on his previous visit, Luke Bartram was standing at the bar talking with his barkeep. At this time of the day the saloon was empty save for the three or four men who worked there.

'Howdy, Jack. Great job you did with the old cannon. What can I do for you?'

'I'm lookin' for someone who might have been in here last night.'

Bartram threw up his hand in a gesture of exasperation. 'You ain't the only one, Jack. Damned feller, name o' Porter, I hired in Cheyenne to deal cards hightailed it out of town afore daybreak. I'm gonna be short of a man at the tables tonight.'

'What's this feller look like?'

'Big build but not very tall. Thin face, bony nose.' Bartram touched his own ear. 'He had bigger ears than most folks.'

Latimer blew air threw pursed lips. He dug into the inside pocket of his trail jacket and pulled out the two mashed slugs, holding them on the flat of his outstretched hand.

'They're .22s ain't they?' Bartram said. 'Porter carried a .22 pistol, same as lotsa gamblers. Where d'you get these?'

'Outa Turner's head.'

'Jesus! You reckon Porter coulda killed Turner?'

'Sure looks like it. He tried to kill Kerswell last night. Where the hell did you hire him, Luke?'

'Owner of the Lazy D, west of Cheyenne, said he was a good man.' The saloon owner's face screwed up with doubt. 'Why would a big rancher do that to me? What the hell does all this mean, Jack?'

Latimer shook his head. 'I ain't sure, Luke. I'm gonna have to study on it.'

★　★　★

'Howdy, Mrs Winslow, I hope Maisie's well,' he said, greeting the woman who had opened the door when he'd knocked at what he still thought of Judge Baker's clapboard in the early evening.

'Good to see you again, Mr Latimer. Maisie's fine. Miss Parkes is in the parlour.'

Latimer pushed open his jacket to unbuckle his gunbelt and hang it on the wooden peg that was at eye-level on the wall a foot from the door.

He followed the woman through the hall of the house and into the parlour where Emma Parkes sat in a soft-backed chair. She wore a silk blue dress that covered her shoulders and reached a couple of inches up her long neck. Around her throat was a string of dark red stones that shone in the evening light showing through the window that overlooked the grassy yard of the house.

'Evenin', Miss Emma. You sure look fine for a small Western town.'

'Thank you, Mr Latimer.' She turned

to Widow Winslow. 'Mrs Winslow, we'll take supper in ten minutes.'

'Yes, ma'am.'

'Do sit down, Mr Latimer,' Emma said when they were alone. 'I must say, I've not seen you like this before.'

A wide grin split Latimer's face. He brushed down his open hand against the material of his jacket, and touched his black silk tie. 'I haven't had these clothes out of my box since I quit the army. No call for 'em in Beaver.'

'You don't attend parties?'

'Oh, sure, but a smart trail jacket an' a clean pair of ridin' pants is all I've ever needed.'

'Then I appreciate your turning out so fashionably dressed.'

Latimer laughed aloud. 'Now I know you're joshing me, Miss Emma. These clothes are over ten years old.' He took his seat on the matching button chair a few feet from her. 'There's somethin' I've been meaning to ask you. You were asking about the Vardon family.'

'Yes, that's correct.'

'You mind tellin' me why you were askin'?'

'Not at all.' She broke off as the door opened.

'Supper is ready, ma'am.'

'Thank you, Mrs Winslow.'

Latimer stood up, and extended his arm, as she rose. 'This takes me back to my army days, ma'am.'

As they went through to the dining-room she looked up at him, a mischievous sparkle in her eyes. 'I've been meaning to ask you about that, Mr Latimer.'

As he pulled back her chair and paused while she settled her skirts, the thought crossed his mind that Emma appeared to have had quite a few questions for him since she'd arrived in Beaver. He took his seat, remaining silent while Mrs Winslow served him with a large plate of soup. He smiled across the table.

'You're interested in the Vardon family,' he prompted, 'an' you were gonna tell me why.'

Emma looked down at her plate for a second, as if gathering her thoughts. 'My father left with his will a letter addressed only to me.' She smiled. 'My brothers were not pleased, but as the letter was not concerned with money they accepted the situation. In the letter my father asked me to travel here and try to find a woman by the name of Sally Vardon.'

'Sally Vardon lived here twenty years ago. Doc Mills knew her. But she left Beaver and she's never returned.'

'Do you know why she left?'

'Doc Mills told me she gave birth to a child out of wedlock. That could have been the reason.'

Emma pressed her lips together, apparently frustrated. 'And took the child with her, I assume.'

'Now that I don't know. I assume she did but I can check with Doc Mills.'

'I'd appreciate if you did — '

She smiled at the very instant the window overlooking Main Street shattered, spraying glass through the room as a round black ball hurtled to where Latimer and Emma sat at the table. Latimer leapt to his feet.

'Firebomb!' he shouted.

As Emma screamed, Latimer bunched his muscles, his hands grasping the corner of the heavy oak table. Sucking air into his lungs he heaved, sending plates and silver crashing to the ground as he pushed the heavy oak table onto its side. At the same time he threw his weight behind the end of the table pushing it towards Emma to protect her from what he knew was coming. An instant later he threw himself behind the table as there was a loud explosion and flames spewed out from the firebomb towards the table behind which he and Emma were sheltering.

His Colt was on a peg in the hallway, too far away to be any good to him at the moment. He grabbed a sharp meat knife from where it had spilled to the floor. If anyone burst into the room it would have to suffice as a weapon. He could hear Emma sobbing at the other end of the long table, but he knew his first priority was to douse the flames that were licking around the furniture before they took hold. He swept up the heavy damask cloth that had been on the table and, risking another attack through the window, darted from behind the table and beat at the flames with the cloth until they were extinguished. Then he turned to where Emma lay on the floor.

Jesus Christ! His heart beat like a hammer. She lay on her back, her eyes closed. From the right side of body protruded a long sliver of glass that must have been blown from the window. Thank God Doc Mills was only in the next clapboard. As he rushed forward to drop to one knee, Widow Winslow appeared at the door from the hallway, her face ashen.

Latimer turned to her. 'Get Doc Mills! Fast as you can.'

He tore a strip from the edge of Emma's skirt, crushing the material into a bundle which he held against the

194

wound caused by the sliver of glass. As he did so, he saw her eyes open. Fear made her almost ugly, her eyes bulging, and her smooth skin pulled taut across her high cheekbones.

'Listen to me, Emma! You ain't gonna die! Doc Mills is on his way. He's gonna get this out. You hear me?'

She gave a little jerk of her head, and he reached forward and took her hand, squeezing it, and despite the sickening worry he felt, he was conscious that she squeezed his hand in return. He remained kneeling beside her, holding her hand. Time seemed to have stopped. Where the hell was Doc? Two minutes later Widow Winslow was at the door again, her face flour-white with worry.

'The doctor's out at the homesteads! He could be a coupla hours yet.'

Latimer thought fast. 'The judge kept whiskey 'round here. Find it!'

He turned back to Emma. 'The glass has to come out.' He looked straight into her eyes for a second or two. 'Now this ain't the time for modesty. You un'erstand what I'm sayin'?'

There was a pause, and then she gave a brief nod, surprising him again by squeezing his hand. Please God, he said to himself, make me get this right. He let go of her hand and scrabbled around in the debris. He found a long steel used for sharpening knives and wrapped it in one of the damask napkins.

'I'm gonna need you to bite on this,' he said. Gently he held it across her mouth as she allowed it to slip between her teeth. 'You bite hard when I tell you to.'

He sucked air deep into his lungs. Then he held the sharp knife that he'd intended to use as a weapon against the material of her dress below the necklace of stones. His hand trembled for a second then he steadied himself. With one deliberate cut of the knife he sliced through her silk dress. He glanced at her face but she had closed her eyes. He laid the knife aside and carefully tore back the dress on her wounded side. When he was satisfied that he had space in which to work he picked up the knife again. He sliced through the material at the base of the glass sliver, before pulling it away from beneath the bundled strip of her dress. The snow-white of her underclothes seemed almost to shine through the dark stains of blood.

'Hold on, Emma,' Latimer urged. 'It'll soon be out.'

Her eyes remained closed but she gave a quick nod. He grabbed a clean end of the damask cloth from the floor beside him and tore off a sizeable strip which he ripped into two pieces. Somewhere at the back of his mind he registered two loud noises from the other side of town but he was intent on what he had to do next.

He pushed forward on one knee to ensure he was in the correct position before he laid the point of the knife on the white top of her underclothes. Then with a deliberate downward stroke he cut through her garment continuing with the point of the knife between her breasts and almost to her navel. The knife still in one hand, he gently folded back the material on the side of her body away from the sliver of glass with the fingers of his free hand. The pale softness of her one exposed breast shone in the evening light as he cut away her undergarment from where the sliver of glass penetrated her body. He laid aside the knife, now blood-stained to its handle. OK, Latimer told himself, this is where she was likely to be hurt really bad. He was aware that Widow Winslow was in the room again.

'Emma, this ain't like a Comanche arrow,' he said softly. 'An' I've got one of them out before. Bite hard now,' he said, and saw her teeth clench.

He pushed aside the blood-soaked cloth around the base of the sliver of glass. The glass had penetrated her body maybe an inch above her breast, now slippery with blood. He wiped his hand down the front of his shirt before pressing his fingers down on her body an inch or two above her breast. She began to whimper behind the napkin-wrapped steel, as his right hand closed around the base of the glass sliver.

'Bite really hard now,' he said.

He felt her heels drum on the floor behind him as his hand slowly, carefully, began to withdraw the glass. Her muffled cries of pain became louder as deliberately he pulled on the glass. Thank the good Lord it was as straight as a bayonet, sliding through her flesh without tearing. He was vaguely aware of his teeth grinding against each other. There! The glass was out! For a second he held it in front of him, before throwing it aside.

'Mrs Winslow! You find that whiskey?'

'Here, Sheriff!' Widow Winslow darted forward.

He took the bottle from her and looked down at Emma. She'd allowed the steel to drop from her mouth and her features had relaxed a trifle but were still marked with a deep frown and screwed up eyes. She said something which he didn't catch, forcing him to lean closer to her.

'Thank you,' she whispered.

'You're gonna be OK, but we got one more job to do afore I finish.' He picked up the steel again, and held it gently to her mouth. 'I'm gonna ask you to bite on that agin, an' then we'll be done. I want you to close your eyes agin.'

He watched her bite down hard, and shut her eyes tightly. He took the cork from the bottle and poured a small amount onto the wound. As she let out a muffled cry he hated himself for hurting her but knew that unless the wound was cleaned immediately it could fester. He scooped up another piece of the damask material and pressed it firmly onto the wound. Then he bound the other strip beneath her arm and around her shoulder, covering the wound and holding the damask pad firmly in place.

'It's finished,' he said. 'An' I hope

you ladies will forgive me.' He again raised the bottle, but this time to his own lips to take a long swallow before ramming the cork back in the bottle.

'Mrs Winslow, I'll find a coupla men to come up here an' clear the mess. You're gonna have to take care of Miss Emma until Doc Mills gets back.'

'I can do that, Sheriff.'

'We gotta get you to bed, Miss Emma, where Doc can see you. Mrs Winslow will attend on you.' He looked down on her and smiled. 'Now I ain't bein' forward, but I want you to put your arms 'round my neck.'

Her eyes opened wide, and for a second Latimer swore he saw amusement register in her eyes. Hell, she was brave as a mountain lion! As he bent his head forward she held out her arms, and he felt her fingers interlock behind his neck. He pushed his hands beneath her legs under her dress, and grasped her around her shoulders. Then he filled his lungs with air, bunched his leg muscles and heaved. A second later he was standing in the middle of the room with her in his arms, her head against his shoulder.

'Show me where I go, Mrs Winslow,' he said.

11

Latimer and Wilson had to wait for daybreak before they could see the full extent of the damage to the jailhouse. The back wall of one of the cages had been blown out, making a hole big enough for a man to crawl through. Around the yard at the rear of the jailhouse, chunks of grey plaster and stones lay scattered across the dirt. The no-goods who'd attacked the jailhouse had used powder for two explosions. They were the noises, Latimer realized, that he'd heard when he was attending Emma Parkes.

'I see you rounded up another Volunteer,' Latimer said.

'Yeah, Hanley stepped forward this morning. Wilkins was carried away on a coupla planks of wood. But he did fine,' Wilson said. 'He managed to gun down the no-good blowing the wall. The body's over with Joe Sterne.'

'What did Doc Mills say about Wilkins?' Latimer asked.

'He said he was gonna be OK but he'd know more this morning.'

'I'll see the mayor an' get Wilkins some extra money.' Latimer looked around at the yard. 'Have a word with Sam from the smithy. He's roundin' up a coupla fellers to work on Miss Parkes's clapboard. He'll know another couple who can make a start here.'

'What I can't work out,' Wilson said, a puzzled frown on his face, 'is why those no-goods broke out Fuller instead o' Will Danton. You think they got the wrong cage?'

'It ain't likely they'd make a mistake,' Latimer said. 'I s'pose Fuller's men could be workin' on their own but seein' as they've joined up with Armand, he ain't gonna have them runnin' loose.'

Wilson shook his head. 'This don't make sense. Armand was all for busting out Danton yesterday. Makes me wonder if there's somethin' we ain't got a handle on.'

'If Miss Parkes had been killed last night Will Danton would have been walkin' outa here this mornin',' Latimer pointed out. 'I reckon that's what Danton was bankin' on.'

But was that what the rancher was hoping for? Latimer was convinced that this latest turn of events did mean that Josh Danton had more cards up his sleeve, and he was about to play them. But despite racking his brains for most of the night while he'd stood guard in the passageway to give his deputy a break Latimer hadn't been able to work out just what those cards were.

'There's mebbe another explanation,' Wilson said. 'Breakin' a man outa jail is gonna fetch the marshal an' his men from Cheyenne and Josh Danton could find himself breaking rocks. But bustin' out Fuller's different. Danton can blame Fuller's owlhoots.'

'But how does that help his son?'

'Mebbe somethin's goin' on even

more important than freeing his son,' Wilson said slowly.

'Then you can bet your last cent that Danton's got Fuller an' Armand joinin' forces. I reckon we're headin' for a showdown, Harry, an' we'd damned well better be ready for it.' Latimer looked up as an excited-looking Jed Morgan from the hotel came across the yard towards them.

'The trail's open, Sheriff! Messenger just got in from Fort Laramie. Mr Kerswell wants to see you.'

'OK Jed, tell him I gotta couple o' jobs to do, an' I'll be over.' Latimer turned to Wilson. 'See Cap'n Bracken, tell him we're gonna need all the men who are ready to stand with us. Seth Williams and his brothers are steady men, have a word with them. I'm gonna see Henry Gibbons, then I'll check on Wilkins at Doc Mills's.' And he could find a couple of minutes to look in on Emma, he realized.

'You don't think Fuller an' Armand will come in today?'

Latimer shook his head. 'I'm hopin' they'll let things settle for a day or so, now they've freed Fuller.'

'You gonna get some sleep? I can handle the place for a few hours.'

'We'll all sleep when this is over, Harry,' Latimer said. 'For now, let's make sure we're ready for Danton's gunslingers comin' in.'

★ ★ ★

'That's mighty good o' you, Mr Latimer,' Wilkins said. 'I'm not gonna be workin' in the mill for a while with a coupla broken ribs. The money's gonna keep us goin'.'

'Mr Gibbons wants you to know he reckons you've earned it. You did damned fine last night.'

'He was darned lucky,' Doc Mills said. 'The cuts on his face look bad but they'll heal in a few days.'

Wilkins grinned. 'Takes more than no-goods with black powder to keep a Wilkins down.' He turned to the doctor. 'How much I owe you, Doc?'

'All taken care of, Mr Wilkins,' Mills said. 'You don't owe me a cent. Now you keep that strapping on until I say you can take it off.'

'Thanks, Doc,' said Wilkins. 'I'll bid you gentlemen good day then.'

Latimer waited until Wilkins had left them. 'He's a good man, coulda got himself killed last night.'

'So could you and Miss Parkes,' said Doc Mills. 'I saw her last night afore I turned in. She'll be fine, thanks to you.' Mills smiled. 'Any time you quit being sheriff you can come and study with me.'

Latimer grinned. 'I'll keep that in mind. Now, Doc, I gotta question for you. The other day you told me more about Sally Vardon. But I got the notion you were still holdin' back.' Latimer saw Mills hesitate and he added, 'I gotta good reason for askin' you.'

And when Latimer heard what Mills had to tell him he couldn't help thinking that the normal life of Beaver

Creek had been turned upside down ever since Kerswell's hired rig had arrived in the town. He left Mills checking his potions, thanked him for his help, and a few minutes later he was being greeted by the two men working on Emma Parkes's clapboard.

'Make a good job o' that,' he said, as he walked up to the door and knocked. Widow Winslow answered.

Latimer touched the brim of his hat. 'Howdy, ma'am. How's Miss Emma feelin' today?'

'You can ask her yourself, Sheriff. She's sitting in the parlour. Miss Emma's a tough one, Boston or not.'

He unbuckled his Colt, hung it on the peg, and followed Mrs Winslow, aware that a big smile was across his face. At the parlour door the woman tapped gently.

'A visitor for you, Miss Emma.'

Latimer heard Emma's voice and then the door was pushed open and he could see Emma in the same soft chair that she'd been seated in when he'd visited the previous evening. He stepped in the room as the door behind him was left a few inches ajar.

'Howdy, Miss Emma. Good to see you up and feeling well, I hope.'

She was pale, he saw, but her face was lit with a smile that shone in her blue eyes. 'I'm fine, Jack,' she said, 'thanks to you.'

He felt really good that she'd used his forename. He saw her touch her shoulder where he could see a bulge below the silk of her dress, and guessed that it was the fresh dressing applied by Mills.

'Can you stay a while?'

'A few minutes,' he said, as she gestured towards the other soft chair. 'I've just heard that the trail to Fort Laramie is open,' he said, sitting down. 'A messenger has arrived an' Mr Kerswell is keen to talk.'

'I'll have to wait for the regular stage,' she said. 'Doctor Mills said I'm not fit enough to travel for a while.'

Another week, he thought, another

week and she'll still be here in Beaver Creek. 'I've something to tell you about the Vardon family,' he said, hoping that what she'd just told him hadn't registered across his face. 'Doc Mills has told me about Sally Vardon. She wasn't a bad girl but she was a mite wild. Anyways, a month after she'd given birth to a boy out of wedlock she upped and quit Beaver, but she left the boy behind.'

'What happened to him?'

'The Williams family took him in. They already had three boys an' said one more wouldn't make a difference.'

Emma's eyes opened wide. 'You mean he's here in town.'

'Sure, he is. Dexter at the livery is a Vardon.'

'The smart young man who came for the buggy?' And then she said something that almost prompted Latimer to drop his hat. 'Sally Vardon took up with my father when he was trying to work the homestead. Then one day she walked out, and my father went back

East. In his later life he bitterly regretted leaving the boy behind. In the letter he left me he asked me to try and find his son. Dexter is my half-brother.'

Latimer leaned against the back of his chair. With everything that had been going on in the town these last days his mind seemed in a constant whirl. He hoped he wasn't losing sight of where his duty rested. He was facing what he knew could be a fight to the death. How had he allowed himself to be so concerned about a visitor from Boston?

'Emma, you gotta remember that boy has only ever known life out here with Seth and his kinfolk,' he said slowly. If by the merest flicker of an eye she made it apparent that she objected to his use of her name he'd apologize, but her expression remained unchanged.

'If you're gonna talk with him promise me you'll step mighty careful.'

'I'll do as you say, Jack,' she said.

* * *

'Sheriff Latimer,' he called, knocking on Kerswell's door in the hotel.

There were a few moments' delay before Kerswell opened the door, and invited Latimer to step in. Kerswell had his jacket off and was obviously working. He waved a hand in the direction of the writing table. 'I was penning a letter to Mr Turner's employers. I hope they will pass it to his family.' He shook his head as if to chase away unhappy thoughts. 'I have to thank you for being gentle with Mrs Mackie,' he said. 'She tells me you were most considerate.'

'Thank you, sir, but I don't reckon you've asked to see me to tell me that.'

Kerswell smiled grimly, and with fingers stained with ink, gestured to more papers spread across his writing desk. 'The messenger carried these from the fort,' he explained. 'They're all I needed to settle the question of the Lazy T.'

'An' what's your decision?'

'My decision, Mr Latimer, is that

Josh Danton is a low-down blackguard who stole his land from the decent people of this country who were looking for homesteads. And when I get back East I'm going to make sure he pays for his crimes.'

Jesus Christ! How much more shattering news was coming his way that day? Latimer turned his hat in his hands, thinking. 'Danton's men broke out Fuller last night. Danton will order Fuller to come after you so he can claim to have clean hands. He's gonna try damned hard to make sure you never reach the railhead at Cheyenne. Now the trail is open we're gonna have to get you out of town as fast as we can.'

Kerswell shook his head. 'It's not that easy, Sheriff.'

'I ain't followin' you.'

'I've now gotta spend some time lookin' at papers held by Abe Wilson.'

Latimer screwed up his mouth. 'Mr Kerswell, why didn't you — ?'

Kerswell held up his hand to

interrupt. 'I've not been wasting time, Mr Latimer, I assure you. Until these papers reached me from Cheyenne I didn't know what I had to ask Abe Wilson for.'

'OK, I'll double the guards on this floor.'

The thought flashed through his mind that if he continued to recruit the Volunteers at this rate, Jess Harper who ran the mill would be down at his office shouting that he couldn't run the business unless he had men available to work. Jess Harper, Latimer decided, was the least of his problems.

'Each time you walk out of this hotel there's gonna be a man with you. No man, an' you don't move from here.' He stared hard at the government official. 'I want your word on that. I don't want you takin' chances. My job is to keep you alive.'

Kerswell nodded. 'You have my word. I'm grateful to you, Mr Latimer. I regret that my being here has caused this town so much trouble.'

Latimer smiled grimly. 'You know something, Mr Kerswell? If we get through this alive it could be the making of Beaver Creek, an' the folks who live here.'

★   ★   ★

Latimer recognized the horse standing at the hitching rail outside his office as soon as he stepped out of the hotel. Josh Danton had lost no time in getting his lawyer, Benjamin Haydn, up from Laramie. Haydn must have left almost as early as the messenger who'd arrived for John Kerswell. But what did Haydn want?

Latimer had tangled with the lawyer once before over one of Danton's men who'd shot up the saloon one Saturday night. Luke Bartram didn't get too ornery over a few fights but a lot of damage had been done in the saloon and Bartram had expected Latimer to take a hand. The drunken cowboy was one of Danton's top wranglers and the rancher wanted him back whatever the cost. Even Henry Gibbons had raised a smile when Latimer had handed him the proceeds of the fine Haydn had paid for the wrangler.

Entering the office Latimer found Haydn seated in front of his desk, sipping coffee that Harry, who leaned against a wall in the corner, must have provided. The lawyer turned towards the door, his eyes in his intelligent face studying Latimer carefully.

'Mr Haydn,' Latimer acknowledged the lawyer as he took his seat behind the desk. 'Thanks, Harry,' he said, as his deputy put a mug of coffee before him.

'You're looking well, Sheriff. I always enjoy visiting Beaver Creek.'

'I'm sure you do,' Latimer said. 'You mind tellin' me why you're here.'

Haydn put down his mug and reached into a pocket within his jacket. He took out a long white document, folded and sealed with red wax.

'May I?' Haydn said, as he picked up

a short knife from the desk and began to cut through the wax. Latimer exchanged glances with Harry Wilson. The lawyer was up to something, that was plain.

'I have here,' Haydn said evenly opening the paper, 'a document that directs you to release Will Danton to my custody, pending any trial. That is,' he added, 'if there is ever a trial.'

'Let me see that,' Latimer said brusquely.

So this was Josh Danton's ace in the hole. He took the document from Haydn and read the left-hand section before turning it over to see the signature and the stamp of Judge Whetstone of Cheyenne. Latimer wondered how much Danton had paid the judge to do his bidding. Or had the judge been approached by other ranchers equally determined that Kerswell would never take the journey back East? He recalled that a rancher had persuaded Luke Bartram to hire the gambler, Porter.

'You agree the document is in order?' Haydn asked.

Latimer nodded. 'I do.'

'Then you can release Will Danton to my custody.'

'No,' Latimer said. 'Danton stays where he is.'

He was conscious of Wilson pushing himself off the wall and staring at him across the office. Latimer ignored him, and continued to stare hard across his desk at the lawyer. Haydn frowned.

'Do you realize what you're saying?'

'I'm sayin' that Danton stays in my jail until a judge reaches Beaver.'

'Are you refusing to obey the lawful order of Judge Whetstone? You will lose your position and go to jail.'

'Mr Haydn. We both know Whetstone can be bought. What you don't know is that Josh Danton is headin' for a fall. He's gonna lose the Lazy T which he stole from honest homesteaders, an' he's gonna spend the rest of his life in jail. When that news comes out I reckon Judge Whetstone might have second thoughts about what he's been asked to sign. He ain't gonna look kindly on a lawyer who put him in a barrel o' tar.'

Latimer had watched Haydn's face slowly grow redder as he spoke, and now the lawyer snatched up the document and thrust it into the inside of his pocket.

'Where did you hear all that nonsense about Josh Danton?'

'From Mr John Kerswell, tasked by General Ely Parker on the instructions of the President himself, to investigate the Indian Bureau. You still doubt my word you'll find Mr Kerswell at the hotel.'

Haydn stood up, his face blotched red and white with anger. 'I heard the mayor of this town once say about you, Latimer, that you could be a mite ornery when you've a mind to. I prefer different words. I consider you a mean-minded sonovabitch. Good day, sir!' He stood up abruptly, turned on his heel and swept out of the office, slamming the door behind him.

Latimer looked across at his deputy, a grim smile on his weather-beaten face. 'I guess I'm the skunk at the picnic agin.'

12

Latimer unlocked the chain that ran through the trigger guards of the long guns stowed in the gun rack. Around him, tense but determined, were half a dozen Volunteers and Seth and two of his brothers. On the other side of the room the desk was piled high with boxes of ammunition. Latimer handed each of the men a Winchester rifle.

'Last time we took these out was for the annual shootin' contest. You all did fine then. You gotta do better this time, 'cos the no-goods comin' in are gonna be shootin' at you.'

Latimer turned to stare hard at the group, his glance resting on each man for a few seconds. 'Mebbe you all didn't sign up for somethin' like this, and some of you have families. Nobody's gonna think any worse of any man who chooses to walk away now.'

Nobody moved, although one or two glanced at their companions alongside. Satisfied, Latimer continued. 'You all know about Danton and the Lazy T ranch. Danton mebbe knows he's finished in the Territory. He could be thinkin' he's got nothing to lose, an' he'll be comin' in for his son. We're gonna be ready for him an' his no-goods but if it don't work out like I'm hopin' then we fall back to the hotel. For the sakes of a lot of folks lookin' to make new lives out here in the West, we gotta make sure that Mr Kerswell stays alive until the soldiers arrive to escort him. You all understand what I'm sayin'?'

'New folks come to these parts an' they'll want to know we're a law-abidin' town,' said one of the men. The others around him nodded, muttering words of agreement.

'One last word,' Latimer said. 'I go down, and Cap'n Bracken takes over.' Latimer looked across at Bracken. 'You OK with that, Cap'n?'

Bracken took his pipe from his mouth. 'That's fine with me, Sheriff, but I ain't gonna be doin' much runnin' about.'

'I'll do the runnin', Cap'n,' Harry Wilson spoke up.

The laughter of the men was interrupted by the door to the street being pushed open. Dexter stood on the threshold looking as if he'd done some hard riding. Dust marked the sweat that showed on his face and on his trail clothes. 'Sheriff! Danton's cowboys are movin' the beef!'

Latimer thought quickly. 'Each man takes two boxes of ammo from the desk,' he ordered. 'You know your places! Get to 'em, an' make sure you got water with you an' carry some grub. This could be a long day. Harry, you stay for a while. An' Dexter, I wanna hear more 'bout what you've seen.'

The men crowded around Latimer's desk to grab their boxes of Winchester shells. Stress showed in their tight lips but each man's eyes showed the determination that Latimer had hoped to see. Dexter stood waiting while the men pushed past him on their way out of the office.

Latimer waited a moment before he faced the young man. 'Dexter, where the hell you been to see beef bein' moved? I tol' you to stay a mile or so from town.'

'I rode out to the Lazy T.'

Latimer grimaced. 'You obey orders next time or I'll kick your butt. You coulda got yourself killed.' Then he got it. 'You been talkin' to Miss Emma?'

'I was out lookin' at our land,' he said. 'The world sure is a great place, ain't it?'

Latimer couldn't resist a smile. 'Sure is, Dexter,' he said. 'OK, go see the mayor an' tell him to spread the word among the townsfolk they should stay in their homes. There's gonna be gunfightin' on Main Street an' I don't want innocent folks killed.'

For a moment Dexter looked as if he was about to ask more questions but he closed his mouth. 'Right away, Sheriff!'

After Dexter had left, Latimer turned to Harry. 'Danton must know that Kerswell's got him in his sights. This time o' the year Danton shouldn't be movin' his beef. He's aimin' to quit the Territory.'

Harry nodded. 'Yeah, I reckon that's it. An' he'll not be plannin' to leave his son behind.'

'Saves us wonderin' when he's comin' in,' Latimer said wryly. 'He's gonna be here any time today.'

'What you want me to do?'

Latimer thought for a moment. With beef being moved at the Lazy T it was going to be tricky to sort out the cowboys from the bunch of no-goods riding towards the town.

'Take the spyglass from my saddle bag an' ride out to the high ground where we put the cannon. You should see when Danton rounds up his gunslingers and starts heading for town. Soon as you see 'em ride like hell back here.' He looked at the old railway clock pinned to the white-washed wall.

'I'm gonna take a walk up to Doc Mills. Might make sense to have him ready to take care of any wounded.'

Ten minutes he was walking up the path to the doctor's clapboard. The two men working on Emma's clapboard were absent. Gibbons, he guessed, had already got the word around town that folks should stay at home. He knocked and after a few moments Mills opened the door. His expression was serious.

'Henry's been over an' told me what's likely to happen,' he said. 'You want me close by?'

Latimer nodded. 'Guess it makes sense, Doc. Sounds as though Danton is pullin' out. He ain't gonna leave without tryin' to free his son.'

Mills nodded. 'I'll see Luke Bartram an' set up in the saloon. Widow Winslow's done some nursin'. Maybe you'd ask her to see me.' A broad smile appeared on his intelligent face. 'Gives you a reason to see Miss Emma again.'

Latimer grinned. 'That plain, eh?'

'Just to me,' Mills paused, his smile broadening, 'and maybe most of the folks in town.'

'I'll see Mrs Winslow for you,' Latimer said.

'You watch yourself today, Jack,' said Mills soberly.

Latimer walked the few yards to Emma's clapboard. The two men provided by Sam Charlton had made good progress. The front of the house was almost back to rights and the front yard cleared of debris. Latimer knocked on the door and waited. Several moments passed by. Maybe Widow Winslow was at the back of the house and hadn't heard his knock. He bunched his knuckles and knocked louder. After a couple of minutes ensued without anyone answering the door Latimer tried the handle. The door was unlocked and he pushed it open.

'Mrs Winslow,' he called. 'Sheriff Latimer here.'

No reply. He took a step forward and

saw the small table overturned in the hall. He felt his insides knot, and his hand dropped to the butt of his Colt as he moved further into the house. After a couple of yards he could hear the muffled cries coming from the cupboard at the end of the hall. Striding forward he heaved open the doors. On the floor, among hanging clothes, was the trussed figure of Widow Winslow. She stared up him, her eyes wide with fear. His heart felt like stone as he bent to tear the gag from around her mouth.

'They've taken away Miss Emma!' she screeched.

For a moment Latimer wanted to grasp her shoulders and shake out of her exactly what had happened. Instead, he took a deep breath and spoke softly as he dropped to one knee and began to loosen the knots in the rope that had been wound around her.

'Did they hurt her?'

She shook her head. 'There was a man with big spurs. He warned the other two they'd pay if she was hurt.'

Armand had his orders, Latimer realized. He didn't have to think too hard what Danton's reasoning was. He planned to ride into town and use Emma as a bargaining chip for Will Danton, calculating that he, Latimer, was the one who'd make the decision for the exchange. He finished freeing the ropes from around the woman and helped her stand.

'We'll get Doc Mills take a look at you. Now don't you worry, we'll soon get Miss Emma back safe.'

After seeing Widow Winslow to the doctor's clapboard he walked back to his office, his mind racing, considering his options. By now Harry would be out on the high ground watching for Danton and his men who surely would come in today. What the hell was he going to do? His stomach lurched at the thought that he could be wrong about Danton's intentions. The rancher didn't need to use Emma as a bargaining chip. If he were to kill her there would be no witness against his son, and Will

Danton would be eventually freed.

Latimer screwed up his mouth. He suddenly realized his bluff about Harry Wilson shooting Will Danton was working in Emma's favour. That's why Armand had been warned that she mustn't be harmed. Danton believed that if he harmed Emma, Latimer would shoot his son. The question, Latimer suddenly realized, he might have to answer. Would he shoot Will Danton if Emma was killed? He breathed a silent prayer that he'd never have to deal with Emma's death. He stepped into his office. Henry Gibbons was sitting in front of his desk.

'I've put the word around town,' Gibbons said. A note of pleading entered his voice. 'But can this business only be settled by gunfighting?'

'There mebbe ain't gonna be any guns,' Latimer said harshly. 'Danton's taken Emma Parkes.'

Gibbons's face dropped. 'Oh, Christ! Will this never end? What you gonna do?'

'I'm keepin' the men in their positions. Danton's finished 'round these parts but he ain't the only rancher who's gonna go down if Kerswell gets back East. If Fuller an' Armand get past us, they'll go for the hotel.'

Gibbons's looked at Latimer. 'You know what you're saying? You exchange Will Danton for Miss Parkes an' you don't change anything. They'll not turn around and leave.'

'I know that,' Latimer said.

Gibbons stood up, pushing back the skirts of his Prince Albert coat. Latimer was surprised to see Gibbons was wearing a gunbelt, the ivory butt of what looked like an old Colt showing at his hip.

'I'm comin' out with you.'

Latimer looked at him, astonished. 'You gone crazy? Danton's bringin' in killers. You ain't gonna last five seconds out there.'

'I'll take my chances.'

'You're gonna get killed!'

'I'm the mayor of this town,' Gibbons

said. He made a noticeable effort to pull back his shoulders, his fingers brushing the lapels of his Prince Albert. 'My place is with you.'

Latimer stared at Gibbons for a few seconds and then stepped forward, his face set. 'I know you reckon you're doin' what's right, Henry, an' I admire you for it. But the town's gonna need pullin' together when all this is finished, an' that's gonna be down to you.'

'But you and young Wilson — '

'This is what we get paid for, Henry,' Latimer cut in. 'An' we got some good men to back us from the Volunteers. Now let's hear no more of this foolishness.' He looked up sharply as the door burst open. Harry Wilson stood at the threshold.

'They're comin' in,' he said tersely. 'Sheriff, I got bad news — '

'Emma Parkes is with them. I know,' Latimer interrupted.

Wilson looked at Gibbons for a couple of seconds before looking back to Latimer. 'What we gonna do?'

'We stick to the plan,' Latimer said. 'But make sure all the men hold their fire. They don't shoot until I give the word or I shoot first. Spread the word. Then it's up to you an' me an' Seth on the street.'

'Right!' Harry said, turned on his heel and hurried from the office.

Latimer turned to Gibbons. 'You do somethin' for me, Henry?'

'Anything you want, Jack.'

'If I don't make it, tell Emma Parkes — ' He stopped.

'I'll tell her, Jack,' Gibbons said quietly.

* * *

'Here they come,' Latimer rasped.

He stood in the middle of the street. Two Winchesters were at his feet, his Colt was in his hand down by his side. He glanced first to his left where Seth Williams, the tall exminer stood taut, his eyes fixed straight ahead. Across his body he held a scatter-gun. By the toe of his right boot boxes of shells lay on the ground.

Latimer looked to his right. Harry Wilson stood with his Winchester held in his left hand, his right hand on the butt of his Colt. His face was pale, and as if aware that Latimer was looking at him he glanced in the direction of the sheriff, and nodded briefly. Latimer returned the nod and looked towards the edge of town where the soft soil of the track gave way to the hardpack of Main Street.

Across the street, seven riders approached in a line, three either side of Josh Danton who rode a big grey. Fuller was to the left of Danton, Armand to his right. On the end of the line was the thin-faced Porter who'd worked in the saloon for Luke Bartram. Latimer swallowed a couple of times. Across Armand's saddle, held hard against him was Emma Parkes. A red kerchief had been tied across her eyes. Below the blindfold her face was chalk white, and as the line of riders advanced towards him, Latimer could see her shoulders were shaking. For an instant he felt obliged to run towards her, gun in hand, blazing away. Then he took a deep breath. He wasn't going to help her by being shot down. The riders reached maybe twenty yards from where Latimer and his men were standing.

'That's close enough, Danton,' shouted Latimer.

'You're finished giving orders, Latimer,' Danton shouted back, as his horse kept walking forward.

Harry Wilson moved his Winchester as a signal, and above the street, from the three buildings that boasted two storeys came the sound of the ratcheting of Winchester rifles held by the Volunteers. Danton immediately hauled back on his reins, and the line of riders halted. Save for Danton and Armand holding Emma Parkes, Fuller and the rest drew their own long guns from their scabbards, looking upwards to where the Volunteers had appeared.

'I told you lotsa times, Latimer,' Danton shouted. 'You ain't keepin' my son in a cage. Nobody here is lookin' to die. We're gonna talk! I got your woman, an' I give you my word she ain't been harmed. But I'm warnin' you now. You don't give me back my son, an' she's gonna die.'

Latimer thought fast. Releasing Will Danton now could be the solution after all. Emma would be freed, and maybe he'd been wrong about Danton still being intent on killing Kerswell. Josh Danton moving his beef surely proved he'd decided to cut his losses and quit the Territory. Kerswell would get back East and not only the Lazy T would be freed up for homesteaders but so would other ranches in the Territory. Hundreds of men and women would have the chance of new lives out here in the west. Who the hell was he, Jack Latimer, to stand on so much principle? Then in one brief instant his careful reasoning was shattered.

'Don't do it, Jack!'

Emma's voice quavered but her words clearly reached him. Maybe she thought he hadn't heard, for she started to call out again.

'Don't — ' Her call was cut off by the sound of a vicious slap.

Latimer's stomach knotted as he heard her cry of pain. 'We'll do a deal, Danton,' he shouted. 'But no tricks! Your son for the woman.'

'It's a deal,' Danton called.

'You an' your men stay where you are or we'll open fire.'

'Let's get to it,' Danton shouted impatiently. He sounded as if he knew he'd won the day. 'I ain't got time to waste.'

Latimer glanced at both Seth Williams and Harry Wilson in turn and then walked slowly towards the jailhouse, his mind churning. He entered the office, picked up the keys to the cage, and went through into the little passageway. Henry Gibbons sat in front of the cage, a scatter-gun across his knees.

'Holland and me agreed he could be more use out there,' Gibbons said.

Latimer nodded, he was beyond being surprised. 'We're gonna do a deal, or they'll kill Emma.'

'Kerswell?'

'I'm gonna chance that Danton's decided to quit the Territory. He ain't gonna worry what Kerswell says back East.'

'You want me to come out with you?'

'No, I gotta do this alone.' He unlocked the door to the cell.

Will Danton stared up at him from where he sat on the edge of the cot, a smirk across his face. 'Shoulda done this a week ago, Latimer,' he said. 'Saved us all a lotta trouble.'

'Get on your feet afore I deliver you to your pa in four pieces,' Latimer snarled.

Danton jumped to his feet, the smirk wiped from his face. Latimer drew his Colt, and placed the barrel against the side of Danton's head. 'You better pray I don't trip steppin' down to the street,' he said.

Beads of perspiration began to

appear on Danton's forehead. 'Hold on, you crazy sonovabitch,' he croaked, 'you want your woman, you walk real careful.'

'Out in the street an' make it slow,' Latimer said.

Together, the two men made their way through the office, across the boardwalk, down the steps, and into the street. All the time Latimer held the gun hard against the side of Will Danton's skull.

'Don't you worry none, Will. I'll soon have you outa this,' called Josh Danton.

'Not so fast. We're gonna do this real slow,' Latimer called. 'You an' your men back off twenty yards. Armand stays where he is. You do that an' the Volunteers up on the buildings will stand down.'

'You go along with that, an' you're crazy,' snarled Fuller at Danton.

'Shut your goddamned mouth, Fuller,' Danton rasped. 'Do as Latimer says.'

'I ain't takin' orders from no hick sheriff,' Fuller barked, bringing up his long gun. His Winchester hadn't reached his shoulder when the slug from Armand's Colt smashed into his skull, blowing him from his saddle. For a second his feet kicked into the dirt of the street and then he lay still.

'We're fallin' back, Latimer,' Danton shouted quickly. He turned his mount's head, as did the other riders, and walked his mount away down the street. Armand sat, staring hard at Latimer over Emma's shoulder. He held his Colt loosely down by his side.

Armand's lips pulled back from his teeth. 'Your move, Latimer.'

Latimer didn't take his eyes off Armand. 'Seth, Harry, fall back.'

From the corner of his eye, he saw the ex-miner back away, still facing in the direction of the line of riders beyond Armand, his scatter gun at the ready.

'Sheriff — ' began Harry Wilson.

'Back off, deputy,' Latimer rasped.

He glanced over towards Wilson and saw him bend slowly, his eyes never off

Armand, as he picked up his spare Winchester, and backed away and out of Latimer's view.

'You get down an' get rid of your horse,' Latimer called to Armand.

For a second Armand hesitated, then he shrugged, and holding Emma Parkes in front of him, stood down from his saddle. He rapped the horse's flanks with the barrel of his gun, the mount heading straight for the water trough fifteen yards distant. The two men faced each other, maybe twenty yards apart, Armand shielded by Emma Parkes, Latimer with his Colt to the head of Will Danton. Beyond Armand, Latimer saw Josh Danton stand in his stirrups to shout down the street.

'Don't you two try anythin' smart!'

Armand didn't take his eyes off Latimer. 'Now what you gonna do, Sheriff?'

'Take the blindfold off her,' he ordered.

'An' if I don't?'

The metallic click of Latimer cocking

his Colt against the side of Will Danton's head sounded along the street.

'For Chris'sakes, Armand,' Will Danton shouted. 'Do as he says.' Armand slipped his left hand quickly up to Emma's head, and wrenched away the kerchief. Latimer could see she was trying to keep up her head, as if to show she was not afraid. But even at twenty yards, Latimer could see fear filming her eyes, and below them, dark patches marking her skin. Yet, he reminded himself, she'd urged him not to make a deal.

'Holster your gun, Armand,' Latimer shouted. 'I'll do the same. Then you set Miss Parkes walkin', an' I'll do the same for Danton.'

Before Armand could reply, Josh Danton shouted. 'Do as he says!'

Armand pulled back his lips from his teeth, and then slowly holstered his sidearm. 'You're makin' this really interestin', Latimer. You know that?'

Latimer uncocked his Colt and slid the gun into his holster, his left hand holding on to Will Danton's arm. He looked across at Armand, knowing that the no-good was planning something. Twice he'd outwitted Armand, and that must be sticking in the gunslinger's craw. Armand was going to try and kill him even if it meant taking a chance with Will Danton's life.

'I give the word, an' you let Miss Parkes go. They're both gonna walk real slow. You try anythin', Armand, an' I'll shoot Danton in the back.'

This time Armand didn't wait for Josh Danton's order. 'OK, Latimer, she's yourn.' He pushed Emma away from him, and she stumbled for a step or two before regaining her balance. Satisfied, Latimer pushed Danton forward.

'Make it real slow, an' no tricks,' he warned.

Save for the cawing of a crow, and the distant barking of a dog no sound could be heard in the street. Both walking slowly, Emma and Will Danton approached each other through the soft soil of Main Street. Halfway between Armand and Latimer they drew level, and both paused to glance at each other before they continued their walk. Latimer drew a deep breath. A few more yards and Emma would be safe. Then his hopes were shattered.

'Run, Will!' Armand shouted.

Latimer saw Armand's hand dropping to the butt of his sidearm. His own hand dropped, and he brought up his Colt, screaming at Emma.

'Down! Down!'

He threw himself sideways, loosing off a shot in the direction of Armand as he saw Emma take a headlong leap forward to flatten herself against the ground. A whoosh of air from one of Armand's shots went past him and a second plucked at the sleeve of his trail jacket as he came up on one knee, pulling the trigger of his Colt, fanning the hammer and pumping shot after shot at Armand. A star of dark red blood spurted from the gunslinger's head, and for an instant Armand stood like a marionette held up by strings before Latimer's final slug sent him crashing backward.

Latimer swung around, to see Josh Danton riding hard towards him and his heart hammered as he realized his Colt was empty. Behind him he heard Harry Wilson and Seth Williams charge forward to join him, but Danton had no weapon, his hand off his mount's rein, held high.

'It's over, Latimer. It's finished,' Danton shouted, as he heaved back to bring his mount to a sudden halt alongside his son who lay at full stretch on the ground. Blood oozed from his head where he'd been caught in the crossfire. Latimer jumped to his feet and raced across to Emma who slowly raised her head from the dirt, her cheeks stained with tears, her eyes still wide with fear.

'You're safe now, Emma,' he said softly. 'You're safe with me.'

13

A smile playing at the corner of his mouth, Latimer sat at his desk looking across at the men of the Citizens' Committee, muttering between themselves and glancing first at himself and secondly at Henry Gibbons. Finally Matthew Epson nodded, and turned to Gibbons.

'Go ahead, Henry. We all agree.'

Gibbons turned to face Latimer, taking from his pocket a long sheet of paper. 'Before I refer to this document, Jack, I'd like you to hear what Mr Kerswell said to me this morning.' With a brief cough he cleared his throat. 'Mr Kerswell wishes it to be known that he thanks the townsfolk of Beaver City for protecting him, and making possible his safe return back East.'

'That's mighty generous of him,' Latimer said.

'He wishes particularly to congratulate the lawmen and the Volunteers of Beaver Creek whom he considers to have done a magnificent job,' Gibbons paused, 'under the leadership of the mayor and the Citizens' Committee.'

Latimer remained expressionless, and inclined his head briefly, to avoid again looking across at Harry Wilson who was leaning against the wall with his mouth open. 'Those are fine words, Henry,' he said.

Gibbons nodded briefly, and flourished the paper in his hand. 'I have here the names for the office of sheriff when the election takes place next month.'

I've survived, Latimer told himself. If someone stands on a platform of peace and tranquillity and garners more votes there'll be other towns in the Territory after folks get talking about what happened in Beaver. He looked at the men in front of him.

'Go ahead, Henry.'

Gibbons looked down at the paper, and again cleared his throat before he began to read. 'Number One. Jack Robert Latimer, presently Sheriff of Beaver Creek.'

Gibbons paused, and looked at Latimer who frowned slightly.

'Carry on, Henry,' he said.

Gibbons's face broke into a broad smile. 'That's it, Jack. Folks in town have told the committee they don't want anyone else. Abe Wilson says it's legal. We can decide you're our sheriff on a show of hands, an' we've done that.'

Latimer frowned. 'Aw, heck! An' I was thinkin' of standin' for mayor.'

Gibbons's face dropped, and there was a moment of total silence in the office. Then the office exploded with laughter, the men of the committee hooting and shouting, slapping each other on the back.

'Sheriff had you danglin' on a line there, Henry,' Epson guffawed. 'Reckon I'm gonna be tellin' my gran'children that one.' He gave a half-bow in Latimer's direction. 'Beaver's a fine place to bring up a family, Mr Latimer, thanks to you an' Harry here.'

There were murmurs of agreement from the men as they filed out of the office. Gibbons was the last to leave. He turned at the door, recovered from all the joshing, and looked across to where Latimer was still seated.

'A fine job well done, Jack.'

'The job ain't finished yet, Henry.'

Gibbons froze, his hand gripping the edge of the door. 'What the hell d'you mean?'

'I'm sayin' the job ain't finished.'

Gibbons screwed up his eyes. 'You gonna tell me about it?'

'Nope. You'll know soon enough.'

Gibbons's face went red. 'You are the most ornery sonovabitch I've ever come across, Jack Latimer. Good day!' Gibbons stepped out onto the board-walk slamming the door behind him.

'Guess you're the skunk at the picnic yet agin, Mr Latimer,' Harry Wilson said, a wide grin across his face.

'Guess so, Harry,' Latimer said. He

glanced up at the clock. 'Dexter should be here in a coupla minutes. You OK with what we're doin'?'

The deputy nodded. 'Sure. I got it nice an' easy.'

Latimer stood up. Through the window he saw Dexter driving a carriage down Main Street, heading for the hotel. He gave a low whistle. In all his time in Beaver, he'd never seen a carriage like it.

'Harry, come an' take a look at what you're gonna be drivin'.'

The morning sun glistened on the polished wood of the carriage. A rear seat, with soft cushions wide enough for two people, was covered in blue silk. The wheels shone with new black and red paint. Latimer opened the door and the two men stepped out to the boardwalk as Dexter went past. He looked in their direction and gave a long wave, a grin on his face.

'Jumpin' rattlesnakes!' Harry exclaimed. 'Mebbe I should wear a tall polished hat.'

'Forget the hat, Harry. You just stay alert.'

The two men headed for the hotel in front of which a group of people had gathered noisily expressing their admiration for the carriage. Dexter jumped down to the street as Latimer and Wilson reached them. The young man held out his long whip to Wilson.

'You don't really need this,' he said. 'Betsy's sweet-tempered. Sure adds a touch of class, though.'

'Where the heck did you get this rig, Dexter?' Latimer asked.

'Seth took it over with the livery. We've had it in the back store for a while. Seth thought it would do Beaver no harm at all if we brought it out for Mr Kerswell's picnic with Mrs Mackie.'

Latimer looked up towards the hotel door, aware that John Kerswell and Dora Mackie had appeared on the boardwalk. Alongside them was Jed Morgan carrying a wicker basket. A bottle protruded from one corner.

'My goodness, Mr Kerswell, this is

magnificent,' exclaimed Dora Mackie, her hand resting lightly on Kerswell's arm. They came down the steps, and Kerswell held out a hand for the long whip.

'My deputy will be driving you, Mr Kerswell,' Latimer said, an easy smile on his face. 'The soldiers will soon arrive from the Fort to escort you.' Latimer bowed in the direction of Dora Mackie. 'With such delightful company it would be easy to forget the hour.'

'You're right, Sheriff,' Kerswell said, as Harry stepped up to the driver's seat. 'Shall we, Mrs Mackie?'

'Thank you, Mr Kerswell.'

When both were settled in the soft cushions, and Jed Morgan had stowed the basket at the rear of the carriage, Harry Wilson glanced behind him.

'OK, Harry,' Latimer said.

Alongside Dexter and Jed Morgan, Latimer stood watching as the carriage drew along Main Street heading for the lake near the homesteads.

'They mebbe ain't young,' Morgan

said, 'but they sure make a nice couple.'

Latimer turned to him. 'I need to talk, Jed,'

Morgan nodded. 'OK, come on up.'

The two men entered the hotel, Morgan taking up his usual position behind the desk. 'So what can I do for you, Sheriff?'

'I want the key to Mrs Mackie's room.'

Morgan's eyebrows shot up to his hairline. 'I can't do that!'

Latimer looked at him a moment. 'Jed, how d'you fancy havin' the most famous hotel in the Territory?'

'Sure I would.'

'Then give me the key, an' trust me.'

Morgan breathed in deeply. 'Mr Latimer, you're the finest sheriff the town could wish for. I just hope you know what the hell you're doin'.' He reached behind him, took down a key, and pushed it across the desk.

Three minutes later, Latimer eased open the door of Dora Mackie's room.

He walked to the window, looked out, and raised the window maybe three inches. Satisfied, he turned back to the room, and quickly searched the drawers in the large chest that stood against the opposite wall.

Save for clothes he found nothing. He quickly opened the long door of the cupboard and ran his fingers down the full length of the dresses and coats. Then he tried the pockets of each garment. Beginning to wonder if he'd made a bad mistake, he looked around the room. A trunk stood in the corner but when he raised the lid he found it empty. He assumed it had contained the clothing in the drawers and in the tall cupboard.

Then behind the trunk he saw a carpet-bag, the flap over the front secured with a brass lock. From the inside of his jacket he took a short sharp knife. There was no going back once he broke the lock, he realized. He breathed in deeply and inserted the sharp point into the hole.

Dexter suddenly threw open the door almost causing Latimer to spill the ink over the paper on which he was writing. That would have been a real shame as he would have had to start again for such an important paper.

'Mr Kerswell's on his way back, Sheriff.'

Latimer stood up. 'Thanks, Dexter. I'm on my way.'

He put on his hat and walked across the street to the hotel. Jed Morgan stood at the door looking as if he'd just robbed the town's bank. Latimer saw the townsfolk on the boardwalks stop and point at the carriage as Harry Wilson trotted the grey down the street towards him while John Kerswell acknowledged the light applause with a doffed hat. A minute later Harry Wilson halted the carriage outside the hotel and stepped down to hand the whip to Dexter.

'Betsy was fine, Dexter.'

Latimer held out an arm to help Dora Mackie down. As he did so, he saw the cloud of dust beyond the edge of town and guessed Kerswell's escort of soldiers was arriving from the Fort. Kerswell stepped down from the carriage in a decidedly good humour.

'You folks here sure know how to look after a visitor. The governor's gonna hear about this.' He turned to Dora Mackie. 'We must prepare ourselves, my dear, for the next stage of our journey.'

'I need to ask some questions first,' Latimer said.

Kerswell turned towards him, a puzzled frown on his face. 'I need to leave, Mr Latimer.'

'And you shall, Mr Kerswell.'

'Then I don't understand — '

'You should prepare to leave, Mr Kerswell.' Latimer glanced towards the edge of town. The blue-coated riders were now clearly visible. 'Mrs Mackie, I have questions I must ask you.'

'Questions?' Dora Mackie gave a

nervous laugh. 'What about?'

'I'll tell you in my office,' Latimer said. He touched the brim of his hat to Kerswell. 'I wish you good fortune, sir, and success with your work.'

For an instant doubt showed in Kerswell's eyes, then he nodded abruptly. 'Thank you, Mr Latimer. I shall mention your name to the governor.'

Five minutes later Dora Mackie was sitting in the chair in front of Latimer's desk. Her face was stiff with anger, and she wasted no time in telling Latimer that she considered being brought to his office like a common criminal an outrage.

'When I speak with my brother at Fort Laramie he will know what to do,' she said sharply. 'You will be hearing from his lawyer.'

Latimer looked at her for a second or two before speaking. 'How long had you worked for Ned Fuller? Were you his woman?'

Her face went chalk white. 'How dare you say that?'

Latimer breathed in deeply. 'Mrs Mackie, Fuller was hired to kill Mr Kerswell. You were working for Fuller. You'd have killed Mr Kerswell if you'd had the chance.'

Dora Mackie looked around at Harry Wilson. 'Are you listening to this nonsense? If you support the sheriff you will pay too. I warn you.' She turned back to Latimer, 'Your foolishness will not end here.' She pulled herself up in her chair. 'Sheriff, I consider myself a good friend of Mr Kerswell. Had it not been for me exchanging rooms, Mr Kerswell might already be dead.'

'The attempt by the saloon gambler Porter, you mean?'

She nodded abruptly. 'Exactly.'

'That was clever, Mrs Mackie, I'll grant you that. You described another one of Fuller's men, obviously known to you, who then disappeared. But Porter could not have got into your room. The window opens only three inches, and needs repairing. The town's carpenter has it on the list he showed me. A man Porter's size could not have got into your room that way, and he didn't pass the Volunteer on guard.'

'He did enter my room, I tell you,' her voice was a croak.

Latimer opened the top drawer of his desk. He took out the .22 pistol he'd taken from the carpet-bag and put it before the woman. 'Turner was killed by a .22. Two shots to the back of his neck. How did you catch a man like Turner off guard? A romantic embrace, perhaps?'

'This is all nonsense.'

Latimer reached into his desk drawer again. 'Not nonsense, Mrs Mackie. I call it greed.' Alongside the pistol he placed the gold ring once worn by Turner and seen to be missing by Latimer when he saw the body on the table at Joe Sterne's place.

'Turner's ring was in your bag with the pistol.' His face set hard. 'My deputy will go with you to the hotel where your effects will be packed. You will be placed in the custody of the officer in charge of Mr Kerswell's escort and taken to Fort Laramie.' Latimer tapped the long sheet of paper on his desk. 'You will be charged with the murder of Frederick Turner, a government agent.'

Before Latimer could make a move, Dora Mackie snatched up the pistol, thrust the barrel into her mouth and pulled the trigger. There was a muffled report. The light in her eyes went out, and she crashed backwards. Latimer knew she was dead before she hit the floor.

'Jesus Christ!'

Harry Wilson stood rigid, his face chalk white, as for a second or two he stared down at the body. He looked at Latimer. 'What the hell we gonna do?'

'Nothing,' Latimer said, aware that he was gripping the sides of his chair so hard his knuckles hurt. He stood up slowly, and looked down at the body. 'She shot herself. That's the end of it. She knew they'd have hanged her down in Cheyenne. You ever seen a woman hanged, Harry? It ain't a pretty sight. Get Joe Sterne here. I'll see Kerswell.'

* * *

Gibbons looked a worried man. 'What did you say to Kerswell?'

Latimer shrugged. 'I explained what had gone on, an' how she'd been playin' with him.'

'Christ, Jack! He was fond of the woman an' you walk into his room and tell him she's just killed herself in your office.'

'He wasn't so fond of her when I told him that she was planning to kill him on the picnic this morning. That's why I had Harry drive them.'

Gibbons lowered himself to his chair. 'There's nothing else is there, Jack? The whole business is really over. I couldn't take any more.'

Latimer grinned. 'No, that's all, Henry. Kerswell's left with the escort. We'll be back to normal tomorrow.'

Maybe almost normal, he reminded

himself as he walked up to Judge Baker's house. The front of the clapboard had been completely repaired. He'd need to mention to Emma that she should give Sam a handsome tip for getting the work done so quickly. He knocked on the door and a moment later it was opened by Widow Winslow.

'Come on in, Sheriff. Doctor Mills is with Miss Emma.'

Latimer took a step back. 'I'll come back later.'

'No, no. They're taking tea in the parlour together.'

He unbuckled his gunbelt and hung up his hat and was led to the parlour door.

'Jack! Do have some tea!'

Emma sat in her usual seat wearing a blue silk dress with white trimmings which made all the dresses he'd seen in Beaver as drab as mourning black. Her colour was high, and the dark patches below her eyes were beginning to fade. She waved a hand towards the chair next to where Doctor Mills was seated, a cup and saucer balanced precariously on his knee.

'I've lots of news for you, Jack.'

He kept his smile on his face. He had news too, but this wasn't the time to speak. 'You sound mighty pleased.'

'I am,' she said firmly. 'I've been settling my affairs with the help of Doctor Mills and Mr Abe Wilson. I'm handing the ownership of my land to Dexter.'

Latimer raised his eyebrows. 'I never saw Dexter as a homesteader.'

'He isn't. He's then transferring the land to — ' she paused, and looked at Doctor Mills.

'Seth's brother, Jake,' Mills said.

'The livery can't possibly support four men, three of whom have families,' she said firmly, 'so new arrangements have to be made.'

Latimer hid a smile. 'Is that right?' he said.

'So Seth and his other brother will work alone,' Emma said. 'The income from the livery will ensure that two of them can support their families very well.'

Latimer frowned. 'But where does that leave Dexter?'

'I was coming to that,' she said. 'I'm told that your Mr Wilson will hang up his shingle when his father decides to quit.'

Latimer nodded. 'I agreed to that when Harry put on the badge.'

'While Abe Wilson was advising Miss Emma on the land he had some news for us,' Mills said. 'He seemed to think that maybe the law was moving a mite too fast for him nowadays.'

What was that word Emma's brothers used to describe her? Wayward, that was the word, he remembered. Latimer decided that Emma Parkes was the most wayward woman he'd ever met and was ever likely to meet. He pressed his lips together in mock seriousness.

'You're goin' to tell me that Abe Wilson has decided to hand over to Harry.'

'How did you guess?' she asked sweetly.

'And Dexter's goin' to apply to be deputy?'

She nodded. 'Only if that's all right with you, Jack.'

For the first time he detected a note of doubt in her voice and was aware that she was looking at him intently. 'He's a smart young feller,' Latimer said. 'I reckon he'll be fine.'

But then he remembered the reason he'd walked here from Henry Gibbons's clapboard. 'Kerswell's left with the hired rig and the soldiers,' he said. 'The regular stage will be here in ten days.'

'I think you'll be ready — ' Mills began.

'The doctor thinks I'll have to stay longer,' Emma cut in, looking sharply at Mills.

'Maybe the stage after that,' Mills said, swallowing hastily.

'Or even the one after that,' Emma said, looking at Latimer, her eyes shining. 'The doctor reckons I may have to stay a very long time. Isn't that correct, Doctor?' She didn't take her eyes off Latimer.

'Oh, yes,' Mills said, now smiling broadly. 'This might take months.'

'Maybe even years,' said Latimer, his gaze holding Emma's and continuing to hold it as the parlour rang with the sounds of their laughter.

THE END

Other titles in the
Linford Western Library:

LAST MILE TO NOGALES

Ryan Bodie

Nogales was a hell town, in the heart of the desert. Its single claim to fame was its band of deadly guns-for-hire who lived there, especially Ryan Coder, whom some saw as the gun king. Yet Coder found his life on the line when he hired out to the king of Chad Valley and was pitted against Holly, the youngest and deadliest gunslinger of them all. Would Coder end up just another notch on Holly's gun?

THE DEVIL'S RIDER

Lance Howard

When vicious outlaw Jeremy Trask escapes the hangman's noose, he rides into Baton Ridge on a mission of revenge and bloodlust. It had been a year since he'd murdered manhunter Jim Darrow's brother in cold blood. Now, along with the sole survivor of the massacre, a young homeless widow named Spring Treller, Darrow vows to hunt down the outlaw — this time to finish him for good. But will he survive the deadly reception the outlaw has waiting?

SHOWDOWN AT PAINTED ROCK

Walt Masterson

When a wagon train is trapped by armed men in Painted Desert, mountain man Obadiah Peabody helps out. He believes they are all just another bunch of pilgrims aiming for California. But among the innocent travellers are the Driscoll brothers — the meanest bunch of owlhoots. Obadiah realises he's got a tiger by the tail when the brothers turn on their rescuer and kidnap his adopted granddaughter. Can Obadiah succeed against seemingly impossible odds? Can he even survive?

MISFIT LIL CLEANS UP

Chap O'Keefe

A senseless killing prevents scout and guide Jackson Farraday from investigating an odd situation in the Black Dog mining settlement. So he tricks Lilian Goodnight into spying at the High Meadows cattle ranch. Lil discovers range boss Liam O'Grady running a haywire outfit, crewed by deep-dyed misfits. She then finds she must rescue an ex-British army officer, Albert Fitzcuthbert, from renegade Indians. And Lil faces ever more problems that only her savvy, daring and guns can settle!

RANGELAND RUCKUS

Randall Sawka

Chet Mitchell's dream was to raise cattle, near the town of Tanning, in a seemingly inaccessible valley. However, landowner Dave Tanning didn't want strangers to ranch land that he felt belonged to his family. And people laughed at Chet's plan to access the valley, which was surrounded by mountains and enormous rock walls. Many had tried, and died. But when Mitchell unveiled his surprise, Dave Tanning had to face a man who knew how to use his head and his guns . . .

THE BUFFALO GUN

Ken Brompton

Arrow Ridge is a cattle town, its ranges owned by Clay Glandon, ruthless boss of the Big Three outfit. Homesteaders are driven off their land by his men. Only Tom Cardigan's outfit, the TT, will fight for what is theirs. Then, armed with a powerful buffalo gun, Will Keever arrives in town. His reputation as a gunslinger brings unease to those fearing retribution . . . Keever's on a mission — and that mission will bring him into deadly conflict with Glandon.